TEN MINUTES
TO TURN
THE DEVIL

TEN MINUTES
TO TURN
THE DEVIL

Douglas Hurd

LITTLE, BROWN AND COMPANY

A *Little, Brown* Book

This edition first published in Great Britain in 1999
by Little, Brown and Company

Reprinted 1999

Copyright © Douglas Hurd 1999

'The Summer House', 'Ten Minutes To Turn The Devil', 'A Suitcase
Between Friends' and 'Helter Skelter' first published in *A Suitcase
Between Friends*. Copyright © Douglas Hurd 1993.
'Seize The Day' first published in the *Sunday Express*, 1993. 'Sea
Lion' first published in the *Daily Telegraph*, 1994. Copyright ©
Douglas Hurd 1994.
Copyright © Douglas Hurd 1993.
'Home To Vukovar' first published in the *Spectator*, 1998.
Copyright © Douglas Hurd, 1998.

The moral right of the author has been asserted.

A CIP catalogue record for this book
is available from the British Library.

ISBN 0 316 85160 4

Typeset in Berkeley by M Rules
Printed and bound in Great Britain by CPD Wales

Little, Brown and Company (UK)
Brettenham House
Lancaster Place
London WC2E 7EN

To the memory
of
Andrew Osmond

CONTENTS

PREFACE

Disraeli finished a full length novel when he was Prime Minister. Since then, for any Cabinet Minister the practice, if not actually forbidden, has become impracticable. But for the junior ranks of ministers the impossibility need not be absolute. The easiest episode of my sixteen years as a minister was certainly the first, when I served for four years as a Minister of State in the Foreign Office under Peter Carrington and then Francis Pym. We Ministers of State were not exactly idle. We sped about the world, explaining, exploring, persuading, listening. But we had virtually no legislation to put through the Commons, and when any matter in our patch reached a certain level of difficulty it could be cheerfully thrust upwards for the Foreign Secretary to handle. Moreover I had in Stephen Lamport a Private Secretary of easy disposition and a literary bent. Together we managed to write a novel, *The Palace of Enchantment*, and coax it through the watchful examination of our Permanent Secretary. Long distance trains and planes are good forcing ground for a novel, particularly if one has a comfortable seat, a glass of wine and a congenial companion.

After 1983 the clouds thickened as I reached the upper slopes of the political mountain. Journeys became shorter and more intense, the red boxes multiplied. There was never any possibility of writing another full novel until I started *The Shape of Ice* after my resignation from the Foreign Office in 1995. But there remained the itch to write something other than minutes and speeches. During these years I began to hatch the short stories published here. The habit has persisted to the present day. Some of these tales are new. Others have appeared in newspapers, but few papers or magazines nowadays find space for short stories of the length which comes naturally to me.

Short stories, or at least my short stories, tend to originate in a particular episode experienced in a particular place. That episode and place are then emptied of their real-life characters and re-peopled by characters of the imagination, with the events adapted as necessary to fit the new population.

Thus we came to know from genial dinner parties over a dozen summers the hilltop eyrie that Ian and Caroline Gilmour inhabit above a hidden valley of Tuscany beyond Lucca. The dinner on the open terrace, always enlivened by the sparring of old friends, was preceded and succeeded by moments of acute danger and fear, as the guests navigated the precipitous and winding ascent. There are no Gilmours and none of their friends in the story 'Helter Skelter', but, as I confessed to them long ago, the villa and the devilish road are theirs. Rather more daring was the origin of 'A Suitcase Between Friends'. In the spring of 1991 my wife and I accompanied the Queen and Prince Philip on their state visit to the United States. For us the most memorable part of that visit was the least official, namely the weekend of leisure spent cruising on the Royal Yacht *Britannia* round the Keys of Florida. This story was published in the *News of the World*. I felt fairly secure, guessing, perhaps wrongly, that few senior members of the Court relied greatly on that paper for weekly instruction and entertainment. Not that the Royal Yacht or any member of the Royal Family or anyone remotely resembling any member of the household appears in this story of a drug smuggler and a naval patrol. What remains from reality is a picnic on a semi-tropical island transformed into an adventure by a fierce and sudden storm. By one means or another, the Court became aware of the story and recognised the storm; but no harm was done.

As the years passed the stories started to touch political life and to play with the conflict of ideas. 'Sea Lion' flowed from a visit to the Falkland Islands, a place so extraordinary in its landscape and its loyalties that it calls out for a story to be devised within it. Much later 'Roaring After Their Prey' was conceived after a weekend at Mala Mala on the edge of the Kruger Park in South Africa. The story stands by itself but it raises a question, unsettled in my own mind, about how far human values can be applied to the care of wild animals in such a resort. 'The Fog of Peace' deals with some of the ironies of Northern Ireland, reaching a climax in Hillsborough Castle. 'Seize the Day' is a light-hearted account of a European Summit held in Edinburgh; such a summit, much more serious, was to be chaired by John Major in December 1992.

Latterly some, though not all the stories, have homed in on a particular political problem, namely that of civil wars. I believe that this is likely to be the most persistent and frustrating dilemma for foreign policy makers into the next millennium. How is it that in Europe these horrors still break out between village and village, family and family? We are not watching the barbarities of drunken savages or of Nazis drugged by a creed, but often of civil servants, middle class educated Europeans who have worked together and belonged, in many respects, to the same society. What does it feel like to live and bring up children in such a disintegrating community? Can reconciliation take shape among so much blood and destruction? What can Britain or other countries usefully do? We are not prepared to do nothing, that is to sit inert by our television screens as the blood spreads on the snow and the funeral processions tear the heart. But neither are we prepared to do everything, that is march in with legions, pacify the warring tribes by force, appoint a governor, and annex a province to some new international Rome. Of all the techniques which lie between doing nothing and doing everything, which works best and at what risk? How do politicians justify such risks to their own peoples, and what is the reaction? Faced with Northern Ireland, Bosnia and now Kosovo many of us have made speeches and television programmes, written books, or indeed sent in troops and planes. (We do shamefully less of all these things when faced with the more numerous and bloodier wars of Africa, because they seem distant and, at present, hopeless of cure.) It is certain that our successors will have to go on mixing the brew of policy afresh as each successive tragedy stirs our conscience.

Through history there has been a place for fiction in political debate of such matters. The novelist can use the imagination to press home a point or argue passionately for a particular outcome. Or, (more relevant in my case) he can point to a predicament of human behaviour without being compelled, as a politician or a leader writer is, to point a dogmatic way out of that predicament.

Some critics who noticed my stories on Bosnia wrote that they seemed acts of penance; with hindsight, they thought, I was showing that we could all have done more to arrest that tragedy. This is not quite so. I cannot be sure, no one can be sure, whether other policies would have worked better, or whether eventual policies could have been put into effect earlier without disaster. It would be perverse to be dogmatic about this either way, though I am clear that some of the alternatives proposed, such as relaxing the arms embargo on the parties, would have prolonged rather than curtailed the disaster.

When Kosovo reached the point of crisis, new ministers in many western countries proclaimed that they had learned from the mistakes of Bosnia. I hoped that was so, for certainly there were grievous mistakes. But as we yet again watched the trail of refugees, the maimed and the bereaved, snipers posing for the camera, a château filled with negotiators, the warring factions barking at each other, as we yet again read editorials pressing for quick decisive intervention, but of course without pain or risk to ourselves, we realised that not all that much had changed.

The fundamental questions remain unanswered. That is why I wrote the four stories here about Bosnia and Croatia, and returned in 1997 to the theme in the full novel *The Shape of Ice* by imagining a civil war in Russia. Of all these short stories I return most often to 'The Summer House', which was published earlier under a different title 'The Last Summer'; and 'Home to Vukovar', which I wrote after visiting the UN in East Slavonia while making the BBC documentary *The Search for Peace* and the book of the same name.

Historical analysis and imaginative fiction are not enemies, as the flood of excellent recent writing of both kinds about Ireland clearly shows. Indeed both may be necessary for the sort of understanding which has to precede reconciliation. To understand is certainly not always to pardon, but outsiders can hardly be effective in helping forward a peace process unless they understand both the authors and the victims of a war.

I hope this does not sound too portentous a note as the opening to a collection of short stories. They aim to entertain in their own right both those who have read this foreword and those who have skipped it.

1
THE
SUMMER HOUSE

'Turn off that rubbish,' said his wife, and Borisav obeyed.

'Where is this place Vukovar?' she asked, for that had been the main story on the TV news.

'In Croatia somewhere.'

'A long way from Sarajevo, anyway. Such stupidities, shooting and killing, and for what? We don't want any of that here.'

Borisav was not sure. In the Forestry Department where he worked the Muslims and Croats were beginning to talk of independence for Bosnia, whatever that might mean. Serbs like Borisav remained silent. Most of them had worked together for years. Promotion, salaries, houses and schools, the occasional foreign trip, these were what they talked about.

Borisav looked through the sitting-room window at his dusty garden. The narrow strip of land, a hundred yards long, stretched down to an outcrop of rock, below which the land fell steeply away to the red-tiled roofs of the village. A large Yugoslav air force transport plane rose from

3

the airport five miles away. The Forestry Department had done well to build these small, two-bedroom houses for its senior employees 20 years ago. Borisav was fond in particular of a gnarled apple tree at the end of the garden, now heavy with unripe fruit, which must have belonged to an ancient orchard demolished when the houses were built.

His other pride was the wooden summer house which he and his neighbour, Mr Tomic, had built with their own hands, straddling their boundary fence. The effort had taken the two of them almost all their spare time last summer. They had held a great picnic in September to celebrate its completion.

Mr Tomic used to smoke his pipe there of an evening, looking out over the village. Sometimes Borisav joined him, preferring a cheap cigar. They were both Deputy Directors, though in different sections of the Forestry Department, Borisav being concerned with plant diseases and Mr Tomic with accounts. They had not been close friends, but the project of the summer house had brought them together.

Borisav's only son, Ivan, aged 13, was meant to use it for his homework. The homework was particularly heavy this term as his form had switched from Russian to English as their second language. But Ivan was an ungainly lad, without many friends, given to kicking a football aimlessly round the garden when not slumped in front of the television. Indeed, Borisav could see him now, hands in the pockets of his jeans, raising clouds of dust as he trundled the ball under the apple tree. Borisav opened the windows to call his son in.

As if galvanised by the sound of the window latch, Ivan gathered himself together and gave the ball a powerful kick. It cleared the fence and struck Mr Tomic's window, but its force was spent and nothing was lost – except Mr Tomic's temper. He burst out of the house by the back door and yelled at Ivan, 'You bloody fool. You Serbs are all the same, good for nothing except breaking other people's property.'

Mr Tomic's belly protruded over the undone top buttons of his trousers. He had a red face, a big moustache which turned down at the ends and a temper which heated and cooled quickly. Mr Tomic was a Croat, but this was the first time that Borisav had heard him swear at Serbs.

Ivan slouched off, hands back in pockets. Mr Tomic saw Borisav for the first time, and began to relax.

'It'll all be better after independence,' Mr Tomic said. It was meant as a joke.

An hour later, just before darkness fell, Borisav wandered down the hill to a little cemetery that lay at the old boundary of the village, separating it from the houses built by the Forestry Department higher up the slope. He often came there because his own house, containing a talkative wife and sulky son, was not the best place for thinking.

A bronze partisan had been erected at the entrance, with fierce eyes and a jutting chin, for ever on heroic patrol through the mountains of Bosnia during the 1941–45 war. On the plinth below was a list of local resistance martyrs. Borisav had lived in the village only ten years, but had heard enough to know that some of those named had died killing each other. There was no point in going into all that. So many lies were told. It was all history now, or so Borisav believed.

Further into the cemetery was a little circle of olive trees that Borisav particularly liked. Under each had once stood a stone, but most of the stones were split and the names illegible. These were the fighters in an earlier war, of which Borisav knew only vaguely. There had been Serbia of course (there had always been Serbia) and the Empire run from Vienna and Budapest, and perhaps Turks, though they had been earlier. He thought of Mr Tomic's remark, about his neighbour of ten years, his fellow Yugoslav, his fellow-builder of the summer house. Was history coming back? But that was absurd. In 1991 reality was the Forestry Department, the journals on plant disease, the intrigues for promotions and postings, Mr Tomic's accounts, Ivan's football matches. Borisav turned his back on the bronze partisan and walked home to his supper.

A year later nothing seemed too absurd. Borisav had watched his country disintegrating every night on television and finally the soldiers had come to his house. They had been there for two hours, six of them, first joking with Borisav, then shouting at him, drinking his brandy, stamping about his house. It was past 10 in the evening before they left.

'Of course you should take no notice,' said his wife. She had been silent while the men were in the house.

Borisav sat miserable in the chair that looked over the garden, twisting a piece of paper in his hands. It was an order, signed on behalf of the President of the Bosnian Serbian Republic, requiring Borisav Mikovic to register at once for military service. The stamp on the order was smudged and the signature illegible. They had left a peaked cap, khaki jacket and trousers in a heap in the corner of the room; also a scuffed pair of boots and an empty ammunition belt. His wife picked up the jacket.

'Poor stuff,' she said. 'It won't even fit you.'

'Where's Ivan?' he asked.

'Working in the summer house.'

His mother always assumed the best of the lad. They both looked and could see that the summer house was empty.

'About the village somewhere,' she amended.

Borisav could not talk it through with his wife. For years there had been nothing much to talk through. She wanted only to resume their dull adequate routine as civil servant and civil servant's wife, to worry again about the state of the road outside their house, her son's clothes, and the rude girl at the supermarket counter. For some days after the fighting began he had continued taking the bus to work in Sarajevo, but the service had stopped and anyway the Forestry Department had closed indefinitely.

There had been no fighting yet in their village, only intermittent mortars and artillery from around the airport. There seemed no rhyme or reason, no campaign, no advances nor retreats. There were rumours, of course, by word of mouth in the village, and by endless radio bulletins – rumours of Serbs massing for a final assault on Sarajevo, of a Turkish army parachuting in to save the Muslims, a Croat force a few miles to the West – but nothing came of any of these. His father, a bank clerk, had told Borisav that the history of Yugoslavia was 60 per cent heroism and 40 per cent lies. In these days Borisav juggled the percentages about in his head.

But another feeling had also begun to form in his mind. It all had to end somehow, and he could not imagine it ending except in success for the Serbs. Others had come later, and of course they had their rights, but at heart this was Serb country and Sarajevo ought to be a Serb city. Borisav was a Deputy Director of Forests, a family man, a man of peace, but peace would not come again until the Serbs too had their rights, and Serb rights were special. He needed a walk to think further.

'You won't do anything stupid?' said his wife, standing between him and the pile of military clothes. That blue dress made in Milan with the silver braid at the neck had once been her best many years ago, but now she used it for housework.

'No, I won't go a-soldiering,' said Borisav. 'And anyway the uniform doesn't fit.'

Outside he almost collided with Mr Tomic, who had lost weight since he had sworn at Ivan 12 months ago, and today was pale and puffy with alarm.

'I was just coming to see you. You must do something about your friends before they kill us all.'

'They're trying to make me turn soldier, but as for killing, I don't think . . .'

'Look, you silly man, look . . .'

A truck swung round the corner of the road on which the two houses stood, then another, then a third, close enough for the Serbs on board to be singing the same chorus. There were four or five in haphazard uniform, standing or sitting on the open back of each truck, crowding round the mortar. The mortars were not bolted down, but slithered noisily as the trucks took the corner. Then there was only dust, and Mr Tomic clutching his elbow.

'They're up at the Director's house. It's swarming with drunken bandits.'

'The army of the Bosnian Republic of Serbia.'

'That's what I said, drunken bandits. You must talk sense

8

with them. None of us here is political. We just want peace.'

'I'll go.' Borisav tiptoed into his house, and took the army cap from the top of the pile of military clothes. His wife was upstairs and did not hear. The cap was too small, and the inside lining greasy with other men's heads. But the badge might save him from a sniper. He set off up the hill.

The Department of Forestry had, of course, built the Director's house at the highest point of the estate, separate from the others and twice as large. The Director, who was a Muslim, had abandoned it a fortnight ago. It looked as if it had been unloved for much longer. The front gate had been knocked from its hinges, and the small circle of grass before the main door pulverised by truck tyres. Two panes of the sitting-room window had been smashed. A rough silhouette of a man painted on the garden wall was pocked with bullets.

The front door was open and Borisav, simulating a military stride, soon found himself on the Director's terrace, overlooking his own and Mr Tomic's house, and beneath them the village itself. A small blue swimming pool, half full of grubby water, also contained a dead sparrow and two Serbs in their underpants. Other soldiers lounged about, armed and half shaved, on the terrace, and two mortars were visible, shells beside them.

The only man smartly dressed wore a major's insignia on either shoulder. Borisav approached him. 'I am Borisav Mikovic, a Serb living in the village below. I came to ask if I could be of service.' He had decided to say nothing of the botched attempt to conscript him, hoping it was made by a different band of marauders. It worked. The major appraised him carefully, then took a list from his pocket.

'Deputy Director of Forests?'

'Exactly.'

'A pleasure to meet you.' They shook hands.

'You came at the right time. Let me explain. Most of these men are fellow-Bosnians. The Yugoslav National Army sent me here to impose some order on them. I am not succeeding, which may become your problem as well as mine. Our main task is to prevent Muslims from out-flanking us. They could take this hill, and then move round to dominate the airport. We must prevent that. But now we have a second task, to safeguard your Serb village.'

'It is a mixed village.'

'It is a Serb village, with Croats and Muslims living in it. Look, clearly marked as such on my map. There is no doubt, if you Serbs are to be safe, the others must leave. Here is the list of names and addresses. It may be incom-plete – the post office was always inefficient. I thought mortar shells delivered by airmail to three or four of these addresses would do the trick.'

Borisav thought hard.

'No need for the mortars. I will tell them.'

The major appraised him again. 'Very well. Unlike some, I see no need to kill. Only to clean the place out. Tell them the Croats and Muslims have a week. We will not attack them as they go.'

'Where should they go?'

'That is for them. The Croat advance posts are not far away – say twenty miles to the west. For the Muslims there is always Mecca.'

'Serbs can rule the village without chasing the others out.'

The major looked hard at him. 'No longer,' he said. 'I will send a man to your house with a radio telephone. Report to me each evening on your progress. At six each evening.'

Behind them on the terrace there was a hustling movement of soldiers towards food. An orderly had brought out a basket piled high with rough bread cut in thick slices, and another of cold meat and cheese. Though the orderly had his back to him, Borisav recognised the set of the ungainly shoulders.

'Ivan,' he called.

His son turned, but there was no expression on his face.

'Your son?' asked the major.

'My son. He should be at his lessons.'

'He is sixteen, old enough for a Serb to fight.'

'He is fourteen. Ivan, come home with me.'

'No,' said Ivan. 'Serbs should be here, before we are all killed.'

'You see,' said the major, 'you are out of date. I also am a little out of date. Advanced modern thinking is with your son and his friends. They would like to massacre the Croats and Muslims tonight.' The two young Serbs who had been in the pool ran shouting along the terrace in their dripping pants, pelting each other in turn with the dead bird. Ivan was writing something on one of the bread wrappers.

'You have educated him well. He can write,' said the major sardonically.

'Please give this to Mother,' said Ivan, civilly enough.

Borisav shoved the note in his trousers without reading it. He was sad, angry and scared in roughly equal proportions. When he got home he found his wife in the kitchen.

11

She seemed not at all surprised by the news of Ivan. She smoothed out the bread wrapper and read the note carefully. Then she went upstairs without a word, leaving his soup half prepared. In five minutes she reappeared with her small, brown, cardboard suitcase.

'I am going to Ivan,' she said.

'But you told me I must not . . .'

'This is different. He is there, and he says they need a cook.'

'What shall I do?'

'There are tins in the cupboard.'

Borisav scooped up the beans where his wife had left them by the cooker and completed the soup. As he drank it, the promised soldier came with the radio telephone and showed him how to use it. Borisav decided that he would start his mission with Mr Tomic, but not till the morning. By then he would have worked out how to explain to people that they had to leave their homes or be forced.

By 11 o'clock Borisav was asleep. The first bang woke him, of course, being louder than anything he had heard before. But by the time he was awake his concern was not the noise but the fact there was no glass in the bedroom window, and much glass on the bedroom floor.

'Mustn't tread on the glass,' he said to himself as he hauled himself out of bed just in time for the second explosion. This was a fraction less loud, but he was in no position to judge. He stood naked in the centre of the room looking through clear air at a garden filled with smoke.

His mind began to work. He found the radio telephone and pressed the button as he had been briefed. The major seemed to be waiting for him.

'I thought you might call. Our agreement stands. That was a mistake. A bad mistake.'

'Mistake?'

'A young Serb corporal heard a few hours ago that his sister had been raped. In Hercegovina, by Croats. She is dead. He loaded the mortars without orders and fired. He is upstairs under arrest.'

'Was it true?'

'The rape? Who can tell? Not much is true. He believed it.'

'Why fire at me?'

'At you? No one fired at you. The corporal claimed that he had chosen a designated target.' A rustle of paper. 'Tomic, the Croat Tomic . . . Ah, yes, I see, your neighbour. Please express my regrets. That is, if . . .'

'I do not know if . . .'

Borisav put down the telephone and pulled on his clothes. The smoke had cleared from the garden. The gnarled apple tree lurched drunkenly across the boundary fence, most of its ancient roots tugged indecently from the soil. The summer house had collapsed, so that no one could have guessed its purpose from its shape. A small crater marked where Ivan had once studied his English.

As soon as he could, Borisav knocked on Mr Tomic's door. His wife and children had gone, he knew, but surely Mr Tomic could not have slept through the attempt to murder him? Eventually, Borisav pushed through the front door. Two minutes later he found Mr Tomic among the ruins of the summer house, calm, apparently untouched, but dead.

Whether he had decided to sleep there because it was cooler or because it was safer could never be known. His house, like Borisav's, was unscathed. His pipe lay unbroken by his side.

Borisav found Mr Tomic's garden spade and began to dig, but the soil was rock hard. He found Mrs Tomic's kitchen matches and a pile of old Zagreb newspapers. The ruins of the summer house burned well and Borisav thought that Mr Tomic would approve of it as a funeral pyre.

Borisav spent the rest of the morning walking to Sarajevo airport. At the entrance, two Canadians in blue helmets barred his way.

'No Yugoslavs,' one said comprehensively.

Borisav showed his military cap and deployed the phrases he had mustered in his mind during the walk. He was a Serb deserter, and they were hot on his heels. If caught, he would be shot.

'Against the rules to let him in,' said one Canadian to the other.

'No rules work here,' said the other.

So they let him in, smuggling him in a truck to the general's headquarters at the heart of the airport. It was a quiet morning for Sarajevo airport, except when the jets roared in with supplies. Borisav was locked in a barrack room, while at least a dozen people discussed his future, which was bound to be irregular.

Eventually, he was ushered up the steps into an RAF Hercules with a group of journalists and a laissez-passer, signed by a French colonel and addressed to no one in particular, they said as they handed it to him.

'This will be totally useless to you. But it's the best we can do.'

Quite how he had managed to talk his way out of the

country he did not know, but here he was at 45, in good health, with a passable knowledge of English, of plant diseases, and of bureaucratic life, and now without encumbrances in the form of family or country. The Hercules rose steeply to get out of range of SAM rockets as quickly as possible.

'Taking a new route this time,' said the RAF steward. 'Peaceful-looking, isn't it?'

It was not new to Borisav, nor peaceful. He soon recognised the spur beneath him, the red-tiled roofs against the thickly-wooded hill, the estate at the top of the village, the tiny blue oblong of the Director's swimming pool, and just below that he strained, but it was no good. Only in imagination could he see the summer house that he and Mr Tomic had built together two summers ago.

2

TEN MINUTES
TO TURN
THE DEVIL

As his fear grew, the fields and smiling villages of Sussex seemed a foreign country. In his sealed car, Richard Smethwick could gain nothing from the crisp October sunshine as he was driven towards Brighton. He had served in Northern Ireland and was now Defence Secretary, so there was no question of his driving himself or being able to open the windows of the armoured Rover. His childhood and his constituency lay in the neat suburbs of north London. Bare downland, even of the gentle Sussex variety, was alien and, as a prelude to the Party Conference, unfriendly.

Richard wondered again if he had been wise to leave his wife behind. His instinct at moments of danger was to look for her. If she had come, he would have to worry about which receptions they went to, whether the stiffeners were in his shirt collar, and the Christian names of his colleagues' wives. She had a knack with words and had already improved the speech with suggestions which he had at first resisted, then quietly slipped in. But not even she would fully understand the fear grabbing his vitals at the prospect of that speech. Even less because of her brother, Charles, whose photograph in Ascot gear stood on her dressing table. Charles had been serving two years ago as a young officer in the army. Then, Richard had just been promoted to the Cabinet, and he and his wife were a good-looking couple in the headlines for the first time. He had snatched a standing ovation from the Conference with an announcement of four new frigates. Caucasia had existed then only as a dim story on inside pages of the heavies, a dispute between unimportant and unpronounceable politicians thousands of miles away.

Now, of course . . . They had driven quickly through the suburbs of Brighton. Across the street from the domes of the Pavilion, Richard could see the first demonstrations, a hundred or so of all ages under the familiar banner of the huge iron weight labelled 'TON' smashing down on caricatures of the Prime Minister and himself. 'Troops Out Now,' they shouted as they saw the Government car. Those nearest it recognised Richard as he passed and their faces changed to concentrated dislike. Two fists banged on the roof. The police driver was experienced and kept going.

'Soon be inside the police cordon, sir.'

The owners of those twisted faces might well last Christmas have been among those shouting for intervention in Caucasia. It was only 10 months since the stories of organised rape, the long lines of refugees, the massacre in the streets of the capital Shevaropol, had led to the Security Council resolution establishing a safe haven and the dispatch of the European force to protect it. It had been a long 10 months. Last week a British Land-Rover had hit a mine just outside Shevaropol, killing a sergeant and three private soldiers, and bringing the British Forces casualty list alone to 96. On the next day, the TON campaign had stopped the traffic in seven big cities for a minute's silence. A dozen relatives of recent casualties were on hunger strike outside the Ministry of Defence in Whitehall. There were similar agitations in France, Germany, Spain and the Benelux countries, indeed in all countries which had sent troops.

Inside the security zone established by the police, the Conservative Party Conference proceeded in artificial tranquillity. Agriculture and the environment that afternoon, the main Conservative Ball that night, defence in a session of double length next morning. The Channel gleamed reassuringly in the October sunlight. A mile out lay Her Majesty's frigate *Orestes*, designated by Richard to deter any attempt either by the Real IRA or indeed the TON to disrupt the Conference from the sea.

As he climbed the steps from the car into the Grand Hotel several dozen cameras clicked, flashed and shouted 'Good afternoon, Mr Smethwick – this way, Mr Smethwick, will you resign if you lose tomorrow, Mr Smethwick?' Inside, the hotel lobby was full of truants from the agriculture debate. Waiting with the room key was his special adviser, the efficient Hugh, who looked after the political side of his job. The two of them moved quickly through the throng:

'Good luck tomorrow, hope tomorrow goes well, we're all behind you.' But of course they weren't.

Richard noticed one distinguished backbencher hurry his wife behind a pillar to avoid any conversation. He entered the lift as if it were a tumbril.

Hugh had opened the incoming letters and stacked them

neatly on the desk in the bedroom, one pile in favour of tomorrow's pro-Government motion, one pile against. The 'No' file was much higher.

'An organised TON campaign,' said Hugh, 'No real significance.' This was Hugh's moment of the year. For 51 weeks he struggled to hold his own as a political adviser against the massed ranks of senior officers and civil servants in the Ministry of Defence. In this one week of the party conference, he was dominant, master of the Secretary of State's diary, constant at his side. Hugh was tall, dark, 30. He had left merchant banking in boredom, and recently discovered the knack of reading Richard's mind without revealing his own.

The two police protection officers brought in the suitcases and put them on the bed. Tea and some rather bright cakes were laid out on a side table. The Secretary of State poured for them both.

'News about tomorrow?'

'No amendment down yet. They may simply vote the motion down . . .'

'But . . .?'

'The whisper is there will be an amendment. Calling for troops out within two months. The long time limit would be put in to catch the waverers.'

'Moved by?'

'Don't know. They can put it in at the last minute in manuscript. My bet is the National Union will accept that it be debated. But they're standing firm on not calling any MPs or Peers. Should be an occasion for party workers from the associations, that's their line.'

Richard nodded approvingly. He would not say so, even to Hugh, but what he most dreaded was a confrontation on the floor with one of the old war horses of the party, tough cynics who had nothing to lose and much to enjoy from humbling an upstart young Minister.

'And the speech?'

'It's there. Revision 3, with the changes you agreed yesterday.' Hugh pointed to a folder beside the letters on the bed.

'What d'you make of it?'

'Reads quite well now.'

'But . . . ?'

Hugh paused before answering. But he was hired to be frank, and Richard counted him as a friend.

'It'll depend on you, not on the text. You can fiddle with it all night, take it to fourth or fifth revision, but in the end you'll either perform well or not. More important to have a good night's sleep.'

'Does that mean you're against putting it on autocue?'

Again Hugh paused. Central Office liked Ministers to use the autocue, in the interests of brevity and good order.

'No autocue this year, I think. That'll give you room for manoeuvre to come and go from the text. The autocue is a prison without bars.'

'I agree. And tonight?'

'You accepted to dine with the *Times* man, 8.30 at Wheelers. That will give you time to look in at the London Area reception first. Of course you could call off *The Times* and they would understand. But . . .'

'I'll stick to it.' As usual Hugh had got it right.

The packets of soap in the bath were absurdly small but the water decently hot. Richard had not looked at his speech for 24 hours. Instead, he took to the bath the minutes of yesterday's Cabinet meeting, which had been waiting for him at Brighton in a black box. It had not been as tough a meeting as he had expected. He had half hoped that faced with the casualties and the public outcry, his colleagues would have turned down his proposal to reinforce the British contingent in Caucasia – perhaps even instructed him to prepare plans for withdrawal. But the French had suffered even worse, the European partners were so far sticking to the agreed plans, the Russians and Americans were still supportive, and the Prime Minister had given a strong lead in favour of the Ministry of Defence paper. The Chancellor of the Exchequer had muttered about expense, but in a routine fashion. The decision was clear there in the minutes.

'The Cabinet took note with approval of the Prime Minister's summing-up and authorised the Secretary of State for Defence to announce to the Conservative Party Conference the decision to send an additional battalion to Caucasia as part of the planned reinforcement of the European Safe Haven Force, together with a contribution of European Fighter Aircraft (EFAs) of which the details would be negotiated with our partners.'

His face was covered with shaving soap when the telephone rang in the bedroom. He wrapped himself in a bath towel and sat dripping on the bed. It was the Prime Minister.

'Don't wish me luck, Prime Minister. Everyone in the hotel has, and I feel terrible.'

'I wouldn't dream of it, young sir. It's a fearsome business. You will find the courage flow into you if you let it. I remember the hanging debates that Home Secretaries had to cope with in the old days, with Margaret Thatcher fidgeting beside them on the platform. Two bits of advice. One, don't hold back when the time comes. Two, forget the speech tonight, and have a good dinner.'

'Thank you, Prime Minister.' He meant it.

Richard gave himself a whisky as he dressed. He disobeyed the Prime Minister's advice and looked at the draft speech, propping it on the table alongside his hairbrushes. It really read quite well. He would have time to memorise some sentences tomorrow. He decided to leave the passage on Caucasia till the end. If the Conference were really worked up by then they might not allow this.

Outside, by the bus stop, beneath his window, someone was playing 'Land of Hope and Glory' on a saxophone, very slowly and out of tune.

By the time he returned at midnight it all looked different again. *The Times* had been hospitable and their political team had gossiped lightheartedly. There had been no attempt to badger or depress him. But as the lobster bisque was replaced by sole and then crème brûlée, as the Chablis was followed by brandy and then more brandy, his heart slowly turned to lead within him. Unsteady now in his bedroom, he thought of telephoning Hugh or his wife, but was ashamed. He glanced at the speech again and it, too, seemed leaden, hopeless. He swallowed an Alka-Seltzer, lay on his bed, and tried the thriller which he had brought with him.

The pages swam queasily before him and he gave up. Damn, how could he have been so stupid. Raucous dance music drifted up from festive Conservatives below. If he shut the window, he would feel stifled. If he left it open, the music would keep him awake. He left it open. Eleven hours to pass before he was on his feet, before the mob began to bay. He was sure it would be a disaster. He dozed, then woke again, thinking it was near morning. But it was only one o'clock by the luminous dial of his watch. Ten hours to go. He thought of the old tag from Dr Faustus:

'*O lente lente currite noctis equi.*

'Ride slowly, slowly, horses of the night.'

Nothing in politics, not the pleasures of hard work in office, the excitement of good conversation, the small vanities of fame, the sense of occasional service, could make up for these moments of lonely fear. It was not as if, in these small hours, he was sure that the policy was right.

'Ride slowly, slowly . . .'

He went to the window, pushed aside the skimpy curtain. A full moon shone on the sea. The man with the saxophone was no longer by the bus stop. The wind had risen since the afternoon and the surface was ruffled instead of metal-smooth. The buildings at the end of the West Pier, cut off by a stretch of water from the rest of the pier and the shore, seemed to float like a dark island alien to both man and nature. There must be a parable there. He remembered the next lines:

'The stars move still, time runs, the clock will strike, the Devil will come . . .'

Would a second Alka-Seltzer keep the Devil and damnation at bay? Richard stumbled back to bed and slept uneasily.

When he woke, Hugh stood beside him in green vest and running shorts. It was his habit to run from Fulham to the Ministry of Defence each morning, and typical of him to keep to this discipline in Brighton. He carried a cup of tea and the summary of the morning press prepared by the Central Office of Information.

'Nothing new from Caucasia. A poor opinion poll. I'll call for you just before eight.'

Sixty-eight per cent in favour of the immediate withdrawal of British troops. In January, 63 per cent had favoured sending them in. The whirligig of time was bringing its revenges even faster than usual. Richard threw the paper aside, told himself that he had no headaches and went to the window. It was grey and blowing hard, with occasional rain in the wind. The West Pier was no longer sinister, just a monument to financial foolishness. Richard was glad that he had two radio and three television interviews before breakfast. They would fill the time, force him back into the argument, keep fear at bay.

'Those were not good,' said Hugh over his kippers when the interviews were over. The Secretary of State had taken no kippers. He rarely asked his advisers what they thought of his performances because that would be unfair. But they knew that they were free to comment. Richard found that their impressions, and indeed his wife's, were often different from his own.

'In what way?'

'Too defensive. Particularly on the *Today* programme. After all, what we are doing is right.'

'Of course.' Richard thought of his brother-in-law, the fairhaired straightforward soldier, now no longer in Ascot rig but hauling convoys of food and medicine through Caucasian mud.

'Then you must aim for more than a verdict of Not Proven. You must come out of your trench, and charge.'

Richard instead retreated into his shell, and the breakfast soon ended. They had done their best, his friends. His wife on parting, the Prime Minister, now Hugh, had all in different ways told him to be himself, as if this was reassuring advice. Now, he had once again to find himself and get that self into action, whatever it was. As he took the lift alone to the hotel bedroom, he envied those of his colleagues who appeared to have no worries. The Foreign Secretary, for example, seemed to enjoy every minute of the Conference, breezing bonhomously from group to group, with never a care for his own speech, yet always speaking adequately.

In his last hour, Hugh's role was simply to keep the world at bay from Room 206 – no maids to make the bed, no colleagues to pay friendly calls, no boxes from the Ministry of Defence, above all no telephone calls. Richard was left alone to wrestle with his draft speech, to break it in until he could ride it easily. Gone were the fears and introspection of the night. The man with the saxophone was back outside, playing the tune to 'Jerusalem'. Richard thought it was by Parry, but was not sure. The man wore a pale mackintosh, and was stooped and bald. He made mistakes, and at each mistake began the melody again from the beginning. Richard wondered how he had penetrated the cordon. He must be either a melancholy delegate or a man from Special Branch in disguise.

Richard walked up and down the room, speaking from the text in his hand, altering it as he went. It was amazing how the rhythms of the spoken sentence differed from the written. This was why officials rarely wrote good speeches. A phrase which looked well on paper could sound absurd in speech. He sharpened up the passage attacking Labour's lack of defence policy. He discarded a joke produced by Hugh, having heard it flop twice in front of the bathroom mirror. He moved Caucasia to the end of the speech. He timed himself. Twenty minutes was too long, since he would certainly want to pick up points from the debate to which he was replying. He cut out a passage on cost efficiency in the Ministry, which the Treasury had been particularly anxious to retain.

This prosaic work of the professional politician kept him calm until Hugh's firm knock on the door. His wife had given him a new and dashing tie for the Conference, white stripes of all sizes dancing on a dark blue sea. He straightened it carefully in the mirror.

'Walk.' The Conference Centre was only two minutes from the hotel. Hugh grimaced.

''Fraid not. TON are in strength at the barricade. The police will have to push you in at the back. By car to the underground car park.'

As they slid in by the side street, Richard could hear the shouting. He knew its rhythm.

'TON! TON! TON for ever!' and then fortissimo, 'Troops Out Now!'

There was a waiting room behind the platform, with coffee and an array of bigwigs from the National Union. The Area Chairman who was to preside over the defence debate was already ashen. He came over to Richard when he saw him enter, and they were joined by David Halifax, the Party Chairman.

'Difficulty's blown up, they usually do,' said the Area Chairman. He had already lit a small cigar, but it was giving him no pleasure. 'Old Southwood's asked to speak. He's got an amendment.' He produced it from his top breast pocket.

'Delete all after "this Conference" and substitute "urges Her Majesty's Government to enter at once into negotiations with a view to withdrawing British Armed Forces from Caucasia within three months".'

'Clever,' said Richard. 'A generous time limit and vague reference to negotiation.'

'A wrecking amendment,' said the Chairman of the Party, who was tough.

'We said we wouldn't call any MPs or Peers,' said the Area Chairman. 'But Southwood . . .'

No one had expected old Southwood to be rebel standard-bearer. He had resigned from the Cabinet six years before, after five years as Lord Privy Seal. In earlier, almost forgotten, times he had been Foreign Secretary for 18 months. White-haired, rustic, old fashioned, stout, he had no enemies, no fixed opinions, and thus a reputation for sound judgment. It would be impossible not to call him.

'We'll have to call him,' said the Area Chairman.

'But not his amendment,' said the Party Chairman.

Five minutes later they filed on to the platform.

The previous debate, on housing, had been lackadaisical and the hall was only half full. Richard sat in the centre of the platform, the Area Chairman on his left, the Prime Minister on his right. He was no longer afraid. He felt the spirit of combat trickle into him as the hall steadily filled.

The beginning was an anticlimax. The Area Chairman announced that he was not going to call any amendments but that, in selecting speakers, he would have due regard for the strong feelings in the Party about the British intervention in Caucasia. This produced an intake of breath but not quite an outburst of protest. The mover of the pro-Government motion on defence policy in general was bespectacled and competent. He had stood for a seat in Leeds at the last election and now held high office in the

Bow Group. He had overdone the research, and the speech, being overweight but worthy, received only respectable applause. He hardly mentioned Caucasia.

Then came a series of routine speeches, gradually homing in on the Caucasian question but, in the manner of academic debate, no blood was drawn and little emotion stirred. Richard could see that the Area Chairman was calling speakers for and against the motion in proportion to the speakers slips handed in, roughly three in favour to two against.

He called a lady from Witney, and Richard saw that on the slip she had simply described herself as 'mother of serviceman'. She wanted to speak in favour of the motion. He at once sensed a turning point. She was dumpy, her hair was over-elaborate for the occasion, and she had never spoken in public before. She spoke for only two minutes. She supported the Government, she supported strong defence, she supported Richard, she wanted to support the motion but could Richard just explain why her son was risking his life far far away in Caucasia, a country neither of them had heard of a year ago.

As she left the rostrum the Prime Minister handed Richard a note: 'Put-up job.' Richard shook his head. He felt she was artless, genuinely questioning. She drew huge applause in all parts of the hall.

The Area Chairman, beginning to fluster, called Lord Southwood earlier than he had planned to speak against the motion. As the old man lumbered to the rostrum in front of Richard, the applause redoubled. He spoke without notes, from a technical point of view poorly, losing the end of each sentence as his voice dropped. But the gist was clear. The French and Germans were all very well, he had often dealt with them in his time, but they were not our natural allies. He had never thought to see British troops back next door to the Crimea, fighting a war almost as incompetently as that one had been fought. No American or Canadian or Australian troops alongside us – just French and Germans and, he believed, a few Italians. And with what aim? No one had explained. We had just drifted into it because of what people had seen on television and read in the newspapers. It was a war conducted by politicians at the urging of journalists but it wasn't the politicians or the journalists who got blown up, it was the young men like Mrs Whitlock's son, though he hoped not, certainly young men like those from his own regiment blown up some days ago.

The red light glowed in front of him as Lord Southwood reached his time limit. He seemed to take it as a personal affront.

'Very well, shut me up. I've said my piece. It's simple,' and then suddenly he shouted:

'End this stupid adventure now! Get our troops out, get our boys home.'

The hall erupted. About a third of the audience rose to give him a standing ovation. Most of the cameras swivelled to follow him back to his seat, but others stayed to catch the expressions of Richard and the Prime Minister. Both were experienced enough to stay impassive, the Prime Minister smiling slightly, Richard scribbling.

Richard hardly listened to the last 10 minutes of the debate. He was conscious that the Area Chairman had let it run away with itself, that the speakers for the motion were heckled, and those against applauded however feeble their performance. The PM sent him another note: 'Watch the hall carefully. Most are waiting. You have it in your hands. Whatever happens, don't hold back.'

It was the longest letter he had ever had from the laconic old man. He hardly needed it for by now he was angry. Angry with Southwood for speaking out of prejudice rather than experience. Angry with the Party for the crude anti-foreign mood in the hall. Angry with his colleagues and himself for letting TON get out of hand.

The debate ended. As the Area Chairman, with a flow of compliments, introduced Richard to reply, six TON banners were unfurled in different parts of the hall. All carried the device of the heavy black weight descending on the cringing figures of Richard and the Prime Minister, and the slogan 'Troops Out Now!' The cameras swivelled again and there were fresh cheers. The desk in front of Richard rose as he rose so that his text was at the right level for his height. The two glass panels of the autocue were bare. He knew how he must start.

'We can hardly proceed, Mr Chairman, until those banners are removed.'

And so they were, after a minute or two of fluster and booing. He had momentarily gained the initiative.

As was the custom, he introduced by name each of the junior Defence Ministers sitting on his right beyond the Prime Minister. This was received without applause, but without interruption, though he caught one shout of 'Get on with it!' Then he told them that he was putting aside two-thirds of his speech. He was not going to attack the Labour Party, because the argument within the Conservative Party was far more significant. He was not going to talk about expenditure and cost effectiveness, because all the money, all the efficiency, in the world could not make up for a lack of will. And lack of will was what he sensed in the hall that morning, at the heart of the Party which through the years had shown that will at its strongest.

It was too easy to sneer at critics. The French had more troops in Caucasia than we had and had suffered more casualties. The Germans had changed their constitution so that they could contribute. Were we losing our will just as they were regaining theirs? He did not believe it. He believed that the heart of the Party and the heart of the country were sound. We had not lost our courage, we were still prepared to work for a more decent world.

He gambled by pausing for applause, having sensed that the audience was listening intensely and without hostility. It came slowly, led from the platform, but gained strength until most were clapping.

'Troops out,' came a counter-cry, from the right, and a final TON banner was unfurled for an instant. But Richard was sufficiently encouraged. He took them calmly through the argument, answering Mrs Whitlock. She was quite right to ask her question. Her son was not directly defending the soil of England, or our empire overseas, or our trade routes, as his forefathers had done through the centuries. He was doing something new, something in a way more daring and ambitious. He was joining with others in an attempt to deal with wickedness and cruelty, to establish decency and order, not just where the Union Jack flew but throughout the world.

He gathered his voice for a climax, his mind at the same time mining and marshalling the words, not from the text, but from his own emotion and experience. The question was whether Britain should join in the attempt or leave it to others. Were we interested in the new chapter, or simply in thumbing endlessly through the old chapters, constantly recalling the past while others shaped the future? He had not become the Secretary of State for Defence in order to serve as curator of a military museum.

A big crash of applause. Then one sentence leaped forward from another. The audience was changing in front of him, some now actively whooping him on, the hostile element silenced. He wondered whether to criticise Lord Southwood personally, but decided this would not work, and was not necessary. Instead he changed gear, slipped back into the persuasions already in his text, as practised that morning before the mirror. The grand moment was over. Rather than re-create excitement, he coasted on to the end in conversational tone, recalling recent visits to the Falkland Islands and to Northern Iraq, calling on the Conference to show its support for our Armed Forces, not just in an annual vote but throughout the year.

So he ended quietly, but had kept alive the memory of the flashpoint of the debate 10 minutes before. The Prime Minister did not immediately rise to his feet, but let the hall take the lead. At least three-quarters rose to applaud, including a good segment who had earlier applauded Lord Southwood. The vote was four to one in favour of the motion and declared carried by an overwhelming majority.

'You turned it,' said the Prime Minister. 'You'll never have a debate like that again. Thank you. It was out of hand. You turned it.'

Richard was congratulated on all hands. Even the fresh round of radio and TV interviews in the purlieus of the conference centre went smoothly. Hugh was almost excited with pleasure. Richard himself felt sweaty from the lights but at ease. There would be other days, difficult days, but this one was good.

He returned to his hotel room for a bath. At reception he ordered a bottle of champagne to be sent up. Notes of congratulation were beginning to appear under the door. The next thing was to ring his wife. He picked up one of the notes, because it was marked 'Urgent'. It reported a telephone call from the Ministry of Defence. His wife's brother, Major Charles Sampson, had been killed that morning by a sniper 10 miles west of Shevaropol. He had died instantly. His wife had not yet been informed. It was thought that the Secretary of State would prefer to do this himself.

3

A Suitcase Between Friends

'Why don't you come with me?' asked Leonora, not for the first time. The week off Florida on Gianni's yacht was proving an exciting success, but that was because of Gianni's good looks and remarkable wealth. A barbecue on the Cayou Costa would include both quite satisfactorily if only Gianni would come. She had seen Jake loading the champagne into the launch.

The little island itself looked enchanting, white sand framed with trees and a red-brick fort on the promontory. But without Gianni it would lose its charm. He had actually clasped her hand on the bridge at dusk yesterday as the *San Cristoforo* manoeuvred its way out of Tampa harbour.

'My dear Leonora, I have all this,' his gesture embraced the yacht, Jake, the champagne, even the 12-year-old boy and his tutor, 'because I never let my business sleep. I told you I have dedicated this afternoon to my business plan for next year. You will swim and drink and grill your steak, while I write in my cabin. I will have the greater appetite for pleasure with you tomorrow.'

She accepted the tone of finality. Men still retreated maddeningly into a world which most women of her generation could not enter. It was the same with her husband, Alaric, and presumably that was why he had become Minister of State at the Department of Transport.

How absurd Alaric looked as he emerged from their cabin festooned with field-glasses and camera, the beginning of a belly looming above his baggy tartan shorts. 'Pleasure with you tomorrow.' She would have to be content with that. She thought of the amazingly beautiful Louis Vuitton suitcase which she had found in their cabin, her initials exciting in gold near the handle, suggesting a future of infinite improper travel.

The launch was just big enough for the shore party. Leonora sat herself next to the red-haired young tutor. He was called David, and it was not necessary to know his surname. His shorts were baggy, too, but reminiscent of the Eighth Army in the desert rather than the Caribbean. Friendly enough under the freckles, but it was hard to imagine that he had any control of Gianni Two, who had stayed on board with his father.

'Well, what shall we see, David?'

'Oh, an osprey, I hope, Mrs Rowallan. It says here . . .' David had brought out a pocket book *Birds of Florida*. At least he was a passionate expert on this subject.

Leonora concentrated on the Fletcher-Hamiltons opposite. She could not see the point in them. Both tall, thin as matchsticks, plain and dull. Gianni had met them at a fishing lodge in Sutherland that spring. Leonora could imagine the Fletcher-Hamiltons in ugly waterproof garments perched for hours in the rain above a beat of rushing brown water. But why ask them to cruise on the *San Cristoforo*?

Leonora and Alaric had not known Gianni much longer than that, but at least they had met at a witty dinner party off the King's Road. Leonora knew that she looked her best by candlelight. She suddenly wanted to know whether Mrs Fletcher-Hamilton, too, had found a Louis Vuitton suitcase in her cabin.

The launch, with Jake at the helm, nosed its way into a lagoon formed between a spit of sand about 100 yards wide and the main shore of the island. They passed close to the red-brick ruins of a small fort built by the Union as part of the blockade of the South. It looked Roman.

'It looks almost Roman,' she said to the freckled tutor.

'No, Mrs Rowallan. 1863,' said David and went back to his field-glasses. She gave up. He would discover eventually that there was more to life than history dates and nesting terns, but she would not be part of the education.

The lagoon was shallow. Jake found a creek up which he could run the launch to the shore. He began to unload the food and drink. Leonora took charge. It was better to recognise that the group had nothing in common.

'Let's all do our own thing while Jake gets the barbecue organised. I suggest we meet here again in two hours.'

The Fletcher-Hamiltons started off to explore the fort. On the way they paused and stooped, collecting sea shells. David disappeared on to the spit with his field-glasses. Jake found brushwood for the barbecue. Leonora found a tree and sat under it with the latest Frederick Forsyth. Alaric took off all his clothes and floated in the lagoon. It was very hot.

She woke, sticky and ill at ease. Alaric was still afloat offshore. Jake slept by a neat bonfire of brushwood. No one else was in sight.

41

Leonora ran down to the lagoon, burning her feet in the white sand. The water was shallow and too warm to be refreshing. Beyond the spit in the real sea, she saw waves breaking, and beyond them again the *San Cristoforo*, large and reassuring out in the ocean, a haven of order and luxury. She imagined Gianni, dark and cool, hard at work in his air-conditioned cabin.

She struck out across the lagoon, crossed the spit and for ten minutes let herself be tossed and thrown in the breakers. Then she began to think of the champagne waiting in ice buckets by the creek.

As she re-entered the lagoon, the water suddenly changed colour. For the first time she noticed the banks of cloud picking up fast above the trees on the island. The scurrying edge of the cloud was bright with a braid of gold, where it had swallowed the sun. The sky and therefore the world began to change quickly. Leonora saw the trees toss in the wind, then the surface of the lagoon ruffle towards her, then the first heavy drops, and a flash of lightning.

She tried to remember if you were more likely to be struck in the sea or on land. She stayed in the lagoon, feeling pleasure as the rain thrashed the water and the thunder rolled. After a minute or two she remembered how she had taken charge of the expedition. She swam back to the boat and the creek. Alaric was already there.

'Put on your clothes,' she said.

'Not much point. They're all wet.'

'Put them on.' And he did.

'We ought to get the party together and go back to the yacht,' she said to Jake. 'No point in a wet barbecue.'

'Stay here till the storm ends. That's the message I've got,' said Jake. 'They'll signal when it's safe.'

'Safe? Then there's danger?'

'No danger if we stay here.' Jake was a tall Spanish-American of indeterminate age, neat even now in a soaked T-shirt and jeans. He seemed to know what he was doing.

'May be the edge of a hurricane. It'll be rough between here and the *San Cristoforo*. We'll stay here till the boss says.'

'Where are the others?'

Leonora imagined young David struck by lightning among the nesting terns. She took Alaric's glasses and swept the spit with them. Rain blurred the lenses and fell so quickly on the lagoon that the spit was barely visible. Then she saw something which made her hand shake.

'Look over there, to the left of that thorn bush.'

Alaric took the glasses and looked, but saw nothing. Nor, after that, could Leonora. But what she thought she had seen was vivid enough. A modest-sized figure in baggy shorts, pursued by two other larger figures and then thrown to the ground. Could she have imagined it just because she had been thinking of David at the moment? In any case, she felt powerless.

The afternoon filled with fear. The *San Cristoforo* was out of sight. Nothing was certain any more. Ten minutes passed, seeming like hours. Jake began baling the rain-water out of the launch. They were all soaked and silent. The thunder died away, but the rain did not slacken.

Then Leonora saw through the murk the outline of a second launch and heard the throb of its engine. The boat came straight towards them with bulky figures visible on board. In parallel two more bulky figures appeared on the shore pushing in front of them two matchsticks which were unmistakably the Fletcher-Hamiltons.

43

Leonora, normally active, even rash, felt paralysed. It was unreal, a nightmare. The boat came alongside. David, hands and feet tied, sat forlorn in the stern. Leonora could see a brighter red spreading from a cut under his carroty hair.

'What the hell . . .' began Alaric, but then a second – and this time human – storm struck them out of the launch.

There were five newcomers in all. With just a word of command they made the party stand together in the shallows beside the launch, and searched them thoroughly. Then they took the launch apart. Everything moveable was taken out and put back. The steaks for the barbecue were individually unpacked and dissected. The champagne bottles were opened in a fusillade of cracks and the contents poured into the creek. Then there was a pause. The rain had stopped and the clouds were beginning to break up. The largest newcomer faced Leonora in her bikini.

'Who is this?' he said, pointing to David.

'He is David, tutor to the son of Signor Gianni Cordovato, owner of . . .'

'And these?'

'Their name is Fletcher-Hamilton. He is a solicitor in Surrey, and they fish for salmon. And my husband here is a Minister in the British Government in London. And who the hell . . .?'

'Jeez,' said the large man. He turned to confer with his colleagues. This took a couple of minutes. Then he came back to Leonora.

'I guess we owe you an apology, ma'am. Captain Ross Benson, U.S. Coastguard. Now let's go.'

'But how . . .'

'Explanation later, ma'am. For the moment enough to say we took you for drug runners. We know there's a transfer planned this afternoon and this Cayou's a hotspot for it. But now we're in a hurry.'

Leonora felt bound to show some authority.

'We can't go back yet to the *San Cristoforo*. Signor Cordovato said we must wait for his signal that it would be safe.'

'Safe?'

'The hurricane . . .'

Captain Benson laughed and turned to Jake.

'So that was it. Hurricane, eh? Tie this man up. It was a summer shower. It hasn't even reached the *San Cristoforo*. Sea dead calm. You'll see.'

They moved with speed. David was untied. One of the coastguards took over the first launch from Jake. Captain Benson travelled with them. The sun emerged as they passed the walls of the fort.

Within three minutes the two launches were out at sea moving towards the *San Cristoforo*. They drove fast, smacking from one wave tip to another. Captain Benson was busy on the radio.

Leonora looked at the *San Cristoforo* through Alaric's glasses, and then looked again. Surely the angle of the yacht had changed, though the launch had not altered direction. No doubt, the *San Cristoforo* was moving. Captain Benson saw the same.

'Do you understand now, ma'am?'

'I can't say I do. How did you . . .?'

'You respectable folk are the cover for this voyage. But he had to have you out of the way this afternoon while the cocaine came aboard. We thought the rendezvous was on

45

the island, but we goofed. It was right there on the yacht, dammit. A cutter came alongside from the Bahamas an hour ago. We've just stopped her on the way home. Clean of course now, but we know the men and there may be enough trace to convict.'

'We shan't catch the *San Cristoforo*.'

'No need. Radio is a wonderful thing. Look.'

And out of the lingering cloud to the west, Leonora could see two grey shapes heading towards them.

'That's your British West Indies guardship and one of ours. They'll catch him whichever way he turns.'

Leonora looked again at the *San Cristoforo*, stern now towards the launches. There, unmistakably on the rail was Gianni Cordovato, holding a suitcase. Both Leonora and Captain Benson saw him drop it into the sea.

'See that, ma'am? Those cases are the latest in neat construction. Fixed for him in Genoa. Some silly girl would be flattered out of her wits by a gift like that. Better still, a respectable wife who'd get it through Customs without a tremor, and then shed bitter tears when it was snatched from her within hours of getting home. Cocaine in the lining and all.'

Leonora said nothing.

Hours later, in their Miami hotel, she said to Mrs Fletcher-Hamilton: 'By the way, did you find a suitcase in your cabin?'

'Yes, it was so beautiful. I suppose now . . .'

Even though she understood it all, Leonora felt a sweet pang of sadness.

4

SEIZE THE DAY

Red, yellow, black – red, yellow, black – but what's the point of getting the Union Jack the right way up if you then mix up Belgium and Germany?

Philip Arabin was short and fair. He put on weight when under stress. In the last ten days he had added ten pounds. Getting the flags in order outside Holyrood Palace was not part of his job, but the responsible official in the summit administration unit had sloped off to some event at his son's prep school.

'Just check the flags at the palace, would you?' he had said in parting. Philip had enough on his hands preparing for the press at the Meadowbank Sports Centre, once again converted for this purpose. His team were dealing with two thousand, two hundred and fifty-six applications for media passes. The journalists were pouring into the airport even now. Tomorrow, the summit conference – and the pandemonium – would begin.

It was probably a Scottish Nationalist in the contractor's team who had deliberately raised the Union flag wrong side up. The Belgian/German confusion must have been just incompetence. It was a raw day and would soon be dark. All over genteel Edinburgh soft grey ladies were brewing afternoon tea. A band of hard yellow light behind the flags marked the crest of Arthur's Seat and, probably, bad weather tomorrow.

A telephone rang in the contractor's hut and Philip was summoned. As he reached for the phone the table tilted towards him and a plastic mug half-full of coffee threatened to spill over a sketch plan of the interpreters' booths now installed inside the palace.

'Just thought I'd let you know,' said a girl's voice. 'A fax in from Escobar City. Ten more names for their delegation. Won't be easy to find rooms for them. Do you think they'd mind Musselburgh?'

Philip swore to himself. Last-minute accommodation was another little thing wished on him by the vanished colleague.

'What seniority are they?'

'Let's have a look.' The girl paused, then whistled.

'Must be a joke. Says here Paola Francesca Cordovez, Prime Minister. Next one, Foreign Minister. Must be someone's idea of fun. The real Prime Minister's already here. Checked in at the Caledonian this afternoon. Professor something.'

Philip was rising quite fast in the Foreign Office because he did not take things for granted. Removing the coffee mug to a safe place, he telephoned the FO's Western European Department. That is how they first learned of the coup d'état in Escobar.

The British Ambassador to Escobar sat in the garden house correcting the draft of his annual report. He prided himself on his punctuality. The report would certainly be ready long before Christmas. London nowadays tended to take these things for granted. They might also suppose that he had an easy task. Quite the contrary. Virtually nothing had happened in Escobar in 1999. Filling four pages of an annual report was thus a work requiring considerable delicacy and skill. The ambassador looked out across the lawn to the yellow facade of his 18th century residence. The declining winter sun sketched the unevenness where the paint was flaking. He would have to bid for repairs again in his next budget. That was always hard going with London. He wished he could move to a neat modern little villa in the suburb the other side of the river where most diplomats now lived. History was a burden.

The telephone rang. It was the head of the Western European Department with news about the fax received in Edinburgh and the first news agency reports. It looked like a coup. The ambassador rose to the occasion.

'I don't have full details yet. The situation here is pretty confused. I'll report again as soon as I can. No, I don't know the woman personally. I'll get back to you as soon as possible.' Then an afterthought, 'As you know, I've felt for some time the political scene here was not as stable as it seemed.'

There had been shouting earlier in the afternoon from trucks careering down the street. The ambassador had assumed they were football supporters. Escobar City was playing a fancied team from the north that afternoon. And perhaps those firecrackers . . .

The ambassador tore up the draft of his annual report. Then, casting aside several of his 59 years, he rediscovered professional energy. The chancery hummed: the ambassador drove fast round the city, saw several of his closest contacts and spoke to others. The agency reports had been correct. He sent a magisterial telegram, personal, to the Secretary of State in London. There had been a bloodless coup. The army and the police had combined to overthrow the Government and install Madame Cordovez as Prime Minister. The embassy, and indeed everyone else, knew only four things about her. She was beautiful, she was unmarried, she was said to be half-Palestinian, and all Escobar enjoyed her highly successful television chat show.

That night, her simple slogans were repeatedly broadcast: 'Time for the people's leader' and 'Banish bureaucrats with Paola Francesca'.

The Foreign Secretary was in no doubt. 'It's clear,' he said, 'that economic policy convergence and the social cohesion fund will be the two themes of Edinburgh. We have to maximise the first and minimise the second.'

They were seated round the Cabinet table at 10 Downing Street in the last half hour of the last meeting of preparation for the summit. John Kettle, the Prime Minister, sighed inwardly. He knew he had been right to promote Martin Pringle, thin, bespectacled and young, to Foreign Secretary. But sometimes he would have preferred at his right hand someone a little less intense, a little less like the efficient Baxter . . . someone who might conceivably have heard of P.G. Wodehouse. He decided on a minute or two of mischief.

'Of course, you and I, Foreign Secretary, know how these summits go.' In fact it would be the Foreign Secretary's first such experience. 'We plan, we calculate, we set the agenda. But then occurs something unforeseen, some thunderclap called X. And the press won't let us think, speak or act anything except X. Tell me, at Edinburgh, what will be our X?'

The Foreign Secretary was nettled and ill at ease.

'I hardly think that this time, Prime Minister . . . for example, last night on *Newsnight* . . .'

'You gave an excellent interview on convergence. But what about the hostages in Lebanon?' For a week now an unknown fundamentalist group in Lebanon, Strength Through Prayer, had been picking up hostages: a Swiss archaeologist from the hills above Beirut, a French aid worker, an eccentric British cyclist and his Dutch girlfriend. No demands yet, no harm apparently done to them, just disappearance and mystery.

'We are doing all we can,' said the Foreign Secretary. 'We are making representations in Damascus as well as Beirut. The RAF in Cyprus is on stand-by to pick them up if they're released. The International Red Cross in Geneva . . .'

'Quite so, quite so. Let us hope all goes well.'

As discussion returned to the convergence policy, the prettiest of the Downing Street secretaries came in with a message. She looked, for a Treasury girl, slightly flustered.

John Kettle read the note and passed it to Pringle. There had been a coup in Escobar. Further report as soon as possible. 'The X?' mused the Prime Minister. 'Or Y? Or possibly even Z?'

At the Caledonian Hotel in Edinburgh only one person was clear whether or not Professor Antonio Darco Platani was still Prime Minister of Escobar. The professor himself was in no doubt. The television in the outer room of his suite showed bonfires and dancing in Escobar City. He turned it off.

'The police will sort out that nonsense tomorrow. I have just talked to the Minister of the Interior,' he announced to the people gathered in the room. He gazed round – two ministers, the Chef de Cabinet, press spokesman, secretaries, newspapers, briefs, the debris of a working lunch. Everything normal.

'Anyone want to leave?'

No one spoke. The spectacles on the professor's nose trembled with satisfaction.

'Then we present ourselves tomorrow exactly as normal. Nothing untoward has occurred. We are the delegation of Escobar. The British are polite and, above all, correct. No one will throw us out unless we ourselves show doubt. You are all resolved?'

'Resolved,' they murmured.

When he had left they turned on the television again. Paola Francesca was announcing the formation of an Anti-Boredom International. 'Telegrams,' she said, 'were pouring in from all over the world.' There was still dancing in the background.

Regretfully, they turned her off and began to put the professor's briefing papers in order.

'In spite of everything she is rather beautiful,' said the youngest member of the Cabinet. 'And amusing,' he added. This was daring, but he *was* the son of the professor's niece and could not easily be removed.

By lunch-time on the first day, Martin Pringle was pleased. As he collected his papers together at the end of the session he caught the eye of one of the kings of Scotland on the wall opposite. They were a job-lot of medieval monarchs, painted in a hurry by a second-rate artist for an early Stuart in urgent need of ancestors.

No one would think it was my first summit, Pringle confided proudly with the king. The first item on the agenda had been the size of the cohesion fund. There had been a satisfactory line of net contributors against the five countries who drew from the fund, and four of the five had scaled down their demands. The total of the fund for the next five years looked like being within spitting distance of the modest figure concealed in Pringle's brief. A dispute which had tormented the Community was almost solved. Only Escobar stood out for more. The professor had not budged from his original bid of £1,200 million. Everyone knew that was because of troubles in Escobar. Everyone sympathised. The Community worked on the principle that colleagues in difficulties at home deserved help – up to a point and within reason. They would find a bit extra for Escobar in the end, but not before the professor had begun to budge downward.

Before his lunch for fellow foreign ministers, Pringle had just enough time to do a *World at One* interview. It would hold the position with the media until evening. The efficient head of his news department hovered at his elbow, proffering a brief entitled 'Bull Points On Convergence and Cohesion'. Pringle liked his staff to be like himself – efficient, quick with detail, preferably thin and bespectacled. The head of the news department passed all these tests. He hovered uneasily.

'Well?' asked Pringle.

'There will be questions about Escobar. And even more about the hostages in Lebanon.'

'I said the interview was to be on the economy only.'

'They know that, but all the news this morning . . . No one at Meadowbank is talking of anything except hostages and Escobar.'

'What's happened?'

'Paola Francesca has left Escobar City. Rumoured to be heading here. Nothing definite. In Lebanon, five more hostages confirmed held by Strength Through Prayer: two Dutch, three Iranian. And a report, unconfirmed, of a Scottish family missing in the area.'

'Family?'

'Young man and his wife, two three-year-olds. Twins . . .'

'What the hell were they doing in Central Lebanon?'

'On their way by car to the triennial philatelic exhibition in Jerusalem. Both of them keen stamp collectors.'

Sometimes Pringle despaired of his fellow countrymen. Jokingly, he ventured: 'Do the twins also collect?' The humour was lost on the civil servant.

'I'm not sure, Secretary of State. I'll check.'

It had rained particularly hard just before lunch, when the guests arrived at the castle. The heads of state and government had been delivered dry to the entrance of the room where they were to eat. The foreign ministers had to dash across a courtyard because the gateway was too narrow for their mini-bus. They were all wet. Nothing substantial was achieved at lunch.

'Better change the afternoon session, I think,' said Kettle. The afternoon session was billed to be on institutional development.

'Change to what?' asked Pringle.

'Hostages.'

'To achieve what?' Pringle had always thought that to change a plan was to show weakness.

'Oh, nothing in particular. Just to avoid being pilloried as useless, irrelevant, out of touch, cruel and heartless.'

The Prime Minister had acquired an early edition of the *Edinburgh Evening News*. The thick black headline read: Summit Plans SAS Rescue Bid. Under a slightly smaller headline, FALKIRK TWINS SNATCHED AT DAWN, were pictures of two boys named Kirkwood. Their grandmother, interviewed at length, was stalwart enough. Their mother and father, pictured wearing shorts and clutching stamp albums, looked bemused.

'But what would be the outcome?'

'A joint appeal, an emissary . . . get your people thinking and drafting.'

'That's nonsense about the SAS?'

'Of course. But as a story, par for the course.'

The Prime Minister asked about Escobar. Pringle explained the latest news.

'Poor Professor Platani. Hasn't done badly by his country. And if being dull is a sin . . .' Then he asked a wayward question to which Pringle had no answer.

'That new Escobar woman, doesn't she have some Arab connection?'

The rain had ceased by evening but the dockside at Leith shone with puddles, stirred occasionally by the biting wind. A floodlight picked out the huge Royal Standard flying above the Royal Yacht *Britannia*. Philip's job that evening was once again not the sort of thing he had joined the Foreign Service for, but it had a certain self-contained satisfaction. The Queen's dinner guests had to arrive in reverse order of precedence, calculated according to the length of time the guest had held office. The Chancellor of

Austria, who had been in office for three years and two months, had to go up the gangway immediately after the Prime Minister of Denmark who had mustered only three years and a day. Since the guests were staying at five different hotels in Edinburgh, the timing of each journey had been nicely calculated to produce the desired result. Philip sat in an office car by the dock gate counting them in. It gave him a thrill to see these great men obediently following his plan. There came Spain, exactly on time, though their drive from the Hilton was one of the longest.

But now something was awry. Three minutes had passed, and no Escobar. The professor had been in office for four years and 46 days. He should thus arrive immediately before the President of France. He should have arrived twenty seconds ago.

Three new black Rovers splashed through the puddles, past the dock gate, on to the quayside. The sudden television glare revealed the Tricolour of France. The President, exactly punctual, was received at the top of the gangway by the Queen.

Two minutes later the Escobar cortège appeared, throwing up even more spray. The front car was travelling so fast that for a moment Philip thought it was bound to end up in the Firth of Forth. It swung round at the last moment and screeched to a halt at the foot of the gangway. A marine opened the door. Out stepped a tall woman of outstanding beauty, in her late thirties, low cut dress in green and gold, diamonds on auburn hair piled high as if in battlements, and on her breast the glinting star of the Sacred Order of St Escobar. The thin crowd clapped, some knowing from the television reports who she was, others simply applauding a show. A gust of wind revealed golden shoes. As the camera lights lit Paola Francesca up the gangway to meet the Queen, Philip radioed to his superior: 'Prime Minister of Escobar a little late, but all guests now arrived.' It was, in a way, the crucial act of recognition.

The professor stormed, but he was powerless. For the new regime, neutralising him had been easy. He and his Chef de Cabinet, loyal, limited, pedantic as his master, had been locked into their hotel rooms and the telephone lines cut. The rest of the staff had changed sides. Tomorrow and the next day would take care of themselves. That night the greatest difficulty had been finding another suite for Madame Cordovez to change in. She had insisted on a full-length mirror.

It was the second and final day of the summit which went into history, but to Philip it flowed inexorably from the first. He had to take the record of Pringle's working breakfast for the other foreign ministers. They wrestled with porridge and kippers, passing from exclamations of polite excitement to full plates quietly pushed aside.

No one from the Escobar delegation attended. Pringle had Escobar top on the agenda. But he could not get his colleagues to focus on the issue. They had all listened to the early news bulletins and seen press summaries from their own countries. Hostages, hostages, hostages . . . that was the story. Strength Through Prayer was picking them up daily, and releasing names and photographs. No response yet from their leader to the appeal launched from the summit the afternoon before. Speculation about the use of military force against the STP in the Bekaa Valley. Speculation about the identity of the STP leader . . . A blurred photograph in three papers of a youngish man with a sharp nose. When his name, Khaled Al-Assat, was mentioned, Philip, sitting behind Pringle, pushed forward on to the table beside the porridge an overnight telegram from Escobar City. The ambassador, still full of autumnal energy, had researched Paola Francesca's Palestinian mother and background. No mention of Strength Through Prayer or Khaled Al-Assat, but he reported her wide acquaintance with several Arab groups. Philip, much daring, had written, 'Worth a try?' against this passage. Pringle considered, frowned, nibbled an oatcake, took out his pen, and scribbled in red, 'Far-fetched.' His sympathies were still with the professor. The breakfast petered out.

In the chair, John Kettle decided, to general surprise, to begin the main session with the cohesion fund. He had his reasons. It would be a test for that extraordinarily fine-looking woman from Escobar who had made such a hit at the Queen's dinner.

She was good company. But he wanted to test her on a real issue. If she continued to ask for as much money as the professor had, then there would be plenty of time later to question her credentials, to parade all these difficulties about legality and the recognition of her government.

Paola Francesca was ready.

A press conference had been arranged and for the third time the hall filled with the extraordinary variety of the Fourth Estate. Reporters in jeans, reporters in dark suits and waistcoats, athletic photographers shoving and shouting, intellectual American ladies, Japanese economists, Hong Kong teenagers.

Pringle's nameplate had been removed from the podium. Only John Kettle appeared.

'Ladies and gentlemen, the conclusions of the summit have been circulated. You have them. Please take them as read. Now I simply want to introduce three new friends . . .'

Paola Francesca appeared in a new, more colourful suit. Then two little boys, reddish hair brushed, freckles scrubbed.

The Kirkwood twins from Falkirk. Safe and sound.

Pringle had been told. Philip had guessed. Strength Through Prayer had released the twins, and all the other hostages, as a result of Paola Francesca's personal appeal. The boys had been flown in from Beirut with their parents by the RAF.

One of the twins had a plaster across his forehead. It seemed that, trying to run away when the kidnappers first appeared, he had tripped and fallen.

There was pandemonium, but no questions were being allowed. Just smiles and the endless clicking of cameras: pictures of joy.

'It is a victory for humanity,' said the Prime Minister. 'A great day for the new Escobar and the new Europe,' said Paola Francesca. A triumph for all.

Later, in the restaurant, at the improvised celebrations, the Prime Minister asked Paola Francesca the question that was at the back of every suspicious mind.

'Did you plan it all? I mean, all?'

She replied simply: 'I didn't know the British had such complicated thoughts. But it all went well, didn't it? No one was bored?'

5
ROARING AFTER
THEIR PREY

'The Duchess of Kent shot a lion across the river there, just this side of the kop.'

Elvira did not grasp what her husband had said. She was watching the baboons playing round the swimming pool below the terrace where the guests of the game reserve sat. But she vaguely caught the royal title. It made no sense.

'In the twenties, or maybe thirties,' explained Luis. 'There is a sepia photograph in the bar. The Governor General brought the Kents up for a week. Helderspruit was the smart reserve even then.'

One of the baboons was sprawling on a white wooden reclining chair near the slope down into the shallow end of the pool. Its infant leapt on to the ornate iron table in front of the chair and began to search its mother's chest for fleas. It was pleasant sitting there in the morning sun. Preposterous of course that one should be so comfortable out in the heart of the South African Veld. Arriving on the airstrip by private plane in mid-morning, they had unpacked in the hut allotted to them. They now sipped white wine waiting for the Land Rovers with the rangers and their clients to return for lunch from the morning drive.

Their marriage had been through a rough patch. They had begun to scratch and quarrel for no particular reason. One day, after a particularly noisy spat, Luis had taken the Mercedes and driven to Johannesburg airport, leaving a curt note to say that he was going to London for a few days, and would be back. Frightened out of her anger, she had telephoned the small hotel in St James's where he usually stayed, but there was no trace. Luis came back as suddenly as he had gone. He offered no explanation but that night they held a peace conference in bed, after making love. One item in the treaty they concluded was a weekend in Helderspruit, away from their friends, his business associates, her bridge partners, their errant servants, the security guards and the clutter of their lives in Sandton. They were childless. She had insisted on comfort if she was to watch animals and was certainly receiving it. It was odd to have to come to the heart of the bush to achieve His and Hers bathrooms. Lunch too would be succulent if the odours wafting from the kitchen behind them were any guide. After lunch, a siesta, and the afternoon game drive beginning at 3.30 p.m.

She glanced sideways at Luis, in the chair beside her. Fifteen years ago she had fallen for the slim ambitious Afrikaner, son of a farmer but determined to thrust himself into the English-speaking fortress of South African finance. Twenty years her senior, he had needed a wife with good connections within that fortress.

The physical side of love had never been of much interest to Luis. In early years she had feared that this indifference meant that he was involved elsewhere. She no longer believed this, but in any case she in turn was now indifferent. Luis was always neat and held himself well. But he had a belly now beneath the trim khaki slacks, his face had coarsened and his hair, though still black, needed careful combing to hide the bald patch.

Because she was no longer in love she no longer had the power to know his mind. The peace treaty had laid down cold-bloodedly that they would make an effort to enjoy each other's company once again, but in any case would stay together. The tensions of marriage seemed to both of them easier to accept than the chores of separation, the tedium of solitude or the search for intimacy with strangers.

The baboons were now engaged in a skirmish of skips and leaps, posturing and grimacing in what must surely be a parody from their observation of human activity – except, Elvira reflected, that none of the baboons could actually have been to a dance in Sandton or to a Capetown garden party.

One thought niggled her.

'Luis, can we find a different ranger?'

The senior ranger John had been allocated to them, and they had already made a rendezvous with him for 3.30 p.m. He was the most experienced of the team. Because Luis had paid extra, John would go out with them alone, leaving incomplete the normal team of four guests in each Land Rover.

'Why? He is clearly competent.'

Luis was reading a text book on antelopes. He was preparing to take the weekend seriously.

'He is plain and middle aged.'

'Don't be silly.' He spoke without rancour. 'Game reserve ranger and gigolo are different professions.'

She was not sure. The Land Rovers were returning one by one across the bridge up the sandy slope into the circular courtyard formed by the huts and administration building of Helderspruit. From each vehicle as it arrived a ranger jumped down and helped his clients to disembark with their cameras, binoculars, sweaters discarded as the sun had strengthened through the morning. The clients chattering enthusiastically about their experiences were of all races, shapes and sizes. By contrast the rangers seemed of a type – fair haired, handsome, courteous, wearing khaki shorts.

But after the peace conference Elvira did not talk in such terms to Luis.

'It might be more fun with someone younger,' she said lamely.

Luis continued to read about antelopes.

As their own afternoon drive got under way, she had to admit that John was a superb ranger. At the outset there was a test of will as they approached the bridge over the river bed.

'I would like to see hippopotamus,' said Elvira. 'I hear they have been seen a few hundred yards upstream.' Over the noise of the engine she leaned forward and used that high, very English voice which she half knew acted as an irritant to most who received it.

John was not irritated. 'Not now. Tomorrow morning,' he said. 'They graze in the early morning. Now they will be wallowing in the pool. Nothing to see but eyes and snout.'

'What time in the morning?'

'We must start out at five-thirty.'

Luis, sitting beside John in the front, glanced back

quizzically at his wife, who on good days in Sandton rose at nine.

The first minutes across the river were disappointing. The Land Rover wound a tortuous way up the slope and into a dense wood. On the slope Egyptian geese pottered in the sun. In the wood were baboons, but Elvira had ticked baboons off her list already. She wondered whether the large sum which Luis had spent on this trip would be wasted. Better to sit at home, vodka in hand, and watch a video of the Kruger. There was nothing attractive in the pitted back of ranger John's squat neck, and if the Land Rover continued to bucket about in this way she would be sick.

Behind her on a raised seat sat the black tracker from the Shangaan tribe, whose skills passed from generation to generation, with his teenage son. The lad wore a brown felt hat considerably too big for him. As they emerged from the wood into open bush, a gentle expanse of long yellow grass dotted with acacia trees, the trackers gave a low whistle on two notes. John immediately stopped the Land Rover and turned off the engine. The tracker pointed to a clump of three acacias halfway up the slope. Elvira could see nothing through the long grass. Slowly John edged the Land Rover off the track and into the bush. It carried a fender in front to prevent saplings and small bushes from whipping back against the passengers. In that way he could make progress without too many deviations. Elvira saw movement under the tree, but could not identify it. The Land Rover was only 20 yards distant when she distinguished two large cats. Something was wrong with the scale of their bodies. Their heads were disproportionately small. One of them extended his body against the tree and began to sharpen his claws.

'Leopard?' whispered Elvira.

From the front seat Luis was scornful. He had been consulting another text book from his rucksack. 'Leopards are the hardest to find. They'd never be out here in the open bush. Smaller, too. Right, John?'

'That's right. These are cheetah, male and female, two years old.'

He edged the Land Rover even closer. The male cheetah continued to sharpen his claws completely unmoved, the bark falling away in strips to the ground.

Elvira found her camera, but the windscreen of the Land Rover obscured the view from where she sat. She stood up. The male cheetah at once gave a short growl. Both animals disappeared. For a second or two waving grass showed where they had passed. Then it was as if they had never been.

'You fool,' snapped Luis.

'I only stood up.'

'Didn't you hear what John said when we started?' She did remember that John had gone through a routine an hour earlier before they crossed the bridge, but she had been too busy organising herself comfortably on the back seat to listen. It had been like a safety announcement at the start of an air journey.

There was no crack in John's calm. He explained again what she had failed to grasp. 'The animals here have no fear of the vehicle. They know it is not good to eat, so they do not approach it. But it has never done them harm, so they do not run from it. Man is different. It is years since a human being killed an animal in this reserve. Except once a lion attacked a foolish client who left camp on foot, and had to be shot. You see, I have a rifle in front of me. You have a powerful cudgel beside you. We are licensed to cull impala when they become too numerous. That is why you will eat venison tonight. Otherwise the animals are safe from us. But they still have a vestigial fear of the human shape and smell. When you stood up, you altered the configuration of the Land Rover. It ceased to be a vehicle only and became involved with their fear of man. So the cheetah ran. They will be a mile away by now. They are the fastest of the cats by far.'

Chastened, Elvira allowed the day to assume a routine which began to attract and absorb her. John constantly exchanged low-voiced radio messages with the other teams out in the reserve. That way they heard of buffalo on the move two miles away.

'It hasn't rained for a couple of weeks. After rain the game is dispersed. They have plenty of pools to drink from. Now it is dry, and they begin to converge on the river.'

They found the buffalo easily enough, sloshing their way through reeds down a drying tributary. Every now and then a beast found a patch of mud still wet enough for a wallow. Sometimes they paused to graze for a few minutes, or to lock horns in desultory fight.

The first giraffe was an excitement, then they became commonplace. The tracker saw elephant, first a lone bull, then another, then females with offspring, but the bushes and trees were too thick for the Land Rover to get close. The sun began to sink and the temperature dropped, for the spring had hardly started.

'Time for a sundowner,' said John.

He set up a little table and produced Castle lager and strips of cured beef on rough bread rolls. This was obviously a personal routine. Luis retired behind a bush. Elvira took close-ups of acacias blurred with the first green, and of a tiny mongoose which posed obligingly before dashing into a conical mound of earth four foot high.

'Termite hill?' she asked, glad that Luis was not there.

'Exactly,' said John, and for the first time there was a current of communication between them.

'Those cheetah, what were they doing under that tree?'

'You did not see? They were just finishing a kill. He sharpens his claws when the meal is over. A dinka antelope. Beautiful, but very vulnerable.'

'If we'd come earlier, would we have saved it?'

'We would not have intervened. We never intervene.'

'Never?'

'In no circumstance whatever. The Land Rover is neutral. It does not interfere with the course of nature. That is why it is respected.'

'So even if something brutal is going to happen, something beautiful is going to be killed . . .'

'We let it happen.'

The chord of communication between them snapped. He was grey haired, too short, stubborn.

'It seems to me that you are a voyeur, a spectator of cruelty. Does it give you pleasure?'

'Mrs de Brundt, when the Governor General and the Duchess of Kent and all the great of South Africa came to shoot lion here in the old days they did it for pleasure, of course. In those days when the lion saw vehicles they melted away in to the Kruger, where they were safe. But the rifles had a purpose. The lion was listed as vermin in the game books. The lion killed antelope, and unless lions were shot, the antelope would disappear. That was what they thought. They intervened with the course of nature. They were judges, not spectators, and their verdict was wrong. Now we do not shoot, and both lion and antelope flourish.'

She felt that he was evading the issue, but Luis reappeared and she broke off. They turned for home. The trunks of dead trees glimmered in white contorted shapes against the dusk. Once again the murmuring radio brought news.

'Two male lions, near our eastern border.'

By the time they reached the lions the tracker had turned on the Land Rover's search light which swept the bush from side to side of the track. Of the four Land Rovers already close to the lions, one backed away as they approached.

'We have another rule,' said John. 'No more than four vehicles at one sighting.'

Elvira felt that even so it was a staged spectacle. They were paparazzi, neutral perhaps but prying. John edged them to within ten yards of the nearer lion, who sprawled at ease under a tree. Unbelievably he took not the slightest notice of the lights. His magnificent head dwindled away into a body that seemed by comparison mean and shrunken. Elvira looked into the lion's eyes – large, yellow, expressionless, except, she thought, for a touch of evil. After four minutes, and for no particular reason, the two lions got to their feet and walked eastward. The Land Rovers followed them through the bush until they crossed the boundary of the reserve.

A fax waited for Luis when they got back to camp, and he was at once on the telephone, stretched on the bed in their hut, talking in Afrikaans to his partner Stefan in Johannesburg. Elvira knew by experience what would follow. She could hardly understand the conversation, which was why Luis had chosen that language. But the outcome was as she expected.

'I have to go. Sasol expects a hostile bid on Monday. Their Chairman has called a meeting noon tomorrow.'

She said nothing. She knew it was no use to plead. She no longer loved him, but since the peace treaty she had learned to accept, even welcome him as her partner for life. He had taken a shower. His brown shoes were a little too smart and polished, and the ornate buckle of his belt gleamed a little too brightly in the light of the bedside lamp.

'You will stay,' said Luis, reaching out to touch her shoulder, obviously relieved that there was no fight. 'I will fly back and pick you up Monday, maybe Tuesday. I will arrange it all.'

After Luis had gone there was one further development. The manager telephoned just as she was settling to sleep with her Joanna Trollope novel. Now that she was alone would she mind changing rangers? He would make no change without her approval, but it would be more convenient for the management if she could join an American couple, very agreeable, and another ranger. His name was Peter. He was younger than John but equally experienced.

It was cold when they gathered in the courtyard at 5.30 a.m. The birds were more insistent in their calls at this hour than later, as if permitted an overture before the animals took centre stage. The humans spoke in hushed voices, sipping hot tea and deciding what sweaters to take. Elvira persuaded herself later that she knew the day would be magic even before Peter introduced himself. His fair hair was bleached by sun, his khaki shirt and shorts were sharply ironed, and unlike the other young rangers he wore stockings which gave him the old fashioned air of a colonial district officer. As the light strengthened she saw the lines on his face which showed that he must be older than she at first thought, thirty-two or so perhaps. When Luis later asked her what they saw that day, she had difficulty. The hippos first of course, two or three already in the big pool of the river upstream of the camp, two others grazing on the bank among the Egyptian geese – huge, looking benevolent but as if they possessed the mix of stupidity and strength that could do great harm. John had told her that they caused more human casualties than any other animal. It was particularly dangerous to find yourself between them and the water.

After that they turned north, then east, following the routines now familiar to her. She sat in the front seat beside Peter, the two Americans in the back. Elephant, giraffe, wildebeest, waterbuck, impala – they saw them all and today she found them full of grace and beauty; even the scuttling warthogs made her laugh. Elvira did not deceive herself, and hardly tried to deceive Luis. Her real study that day was Peter's nose and chin in profile beside her, the schoolboy floppiness of his hair, contrasting with the grown-up tan of forearm and knee. Peter drove less neatly than John and was less communicative. The elderly American couple too were more silent than Elvira had dared to hope. The husband wore a lumberjack shirt and rough corduroys, but had the air of an academic. His wife lacked an air of any kind. The morning passed for Elvira in a silent happy haze.

It was the custom for each team to lunch together on the terrace overlooking swimming pool and river. Elvira rather dreaded this occasion. The silence of the Land Rover had been entirely welcome to her, but equivalent silence at the lunch table would be more difficult. She need not have worried.

'Tell me, do you believe in a higher power?' asked the American professor over the opening fish salad. He had by now introduced himself as Dr Mountfort.

It was not clear whether he was asking Elvira or Peter. Peter said nothing; he was eating a mountain of salad.

'Yes, I think so,' said Elvira.

'This morning must have made you think of the purpose of life,' said Dr Mountfort.

Yes, indeed, thought Elvira, but what if I conclude that the purpose of life is a young man's profile? She was on her second glass of Stellenbosch white.

'These animals beyond the river spending all their time walking, sniffing, running – year after year coping with danger. Their aim is to survive. But in the end they do not survive. Another animal eats them or they die alone in a thicket. What is the purpose of all the strenuous activity which we have glimpsed this morning?'

'I suppose to reproduce, to prolong the species?' said Elvira.

'Yes, indeed, but you must see that only postpones the question. They breed, they protect their offspring. But what is the purpose of those offspring? Do they too exist only to watch, to give warning calls, to fight among themselves, to run from danger, to maul and be mauled?'

They helped themselves to chicken and home-grown vegetables.

'There is an order in what we have seen, all these rela-tionships between species, the pluses and minuses with which each is equipped, all so sophisticated that it cannot be accidental,' said Dr Mountfort, who had taken only a small helping of chicken. 'So there must be a creator, and a plan. The creator must presumably survey the creation he has made. Has he perhaps distinguished man so that we intervene on his behalf?'

'No,' said Peter rather loudly. 'He threw the dice once and let the results follow. When we intervene we make a mess of it. We are not God.'

'No indeed,' said Dr Mountfort.

They prepared for ice cream. The conversation petered out. Elvira would have liked to pursue it, but with Peter alone. Was he following John's doctrine of neutrality in the bush? She hoped he was more warm-blooded. But she could not cope with Dr Mountfort. She could see that he was not booming emptily; he was genuinely looking for an answer. But they all, even Dr Mountfort at Stanford University, even money-making Luis, even Peter daily confronted with creation, saw through a glass darkly.

The afternoon drive showed less game. Elvira tried to draw Peter out about his past and his private life, asking questions in low tones so that the Mountforts in the back seat were not involved. Peter was the son of a Rhodesian farmer who had, to use the phrase of the day, 'taken the bridge' into South Africa as the regime of Ian Smith crumbled in the late seventies. Luckier than most he had managed to smuggle out his money to buy a small sugar farm in Natal, which Peter's elder brother now ran. Peter preferred the more open life of a ranger. That was as far as she got.

'You are not married? Do you have a girlfriend?' As she asked Elvira knew that his physical appeal was clouding her judgement. She was piling on the questions too fast. And so it proved.

'Even a ranger is entitled to a private life, Mrs de Brundt.'

Peter did not pause for a formal sundowner as John had done. He was scouring the bush for a pack of wild dog which had been reported by a tracker but not yet found by any of the Land Rovers. They paused just as the sun was setting by a line of mounds, the wrong shape for termite hills.

'Cattle graves,' said Peter. 'They tried to farm here in the twenties. It didn't work. Malaria wrecked the cattle-men. Lions ate the cattle.' He made it sound like a success. Nature had triumphed. Against the last glimmer from the sun a bird launched from a tree planted by one of the mounds a long trembling appeal. Peter listened carefully, then repeated the song exactly, cupping his mouth with his hands. The bird responded to the call and flew to a closer tree. 'Look,' he said, handing Elvira his binoculars. Their hands touched, but this might have been by accident. It was a tiny white owl with staring round face.

'Can John do that?' she asked.

'I don't know.'

There was no doubt about the next time. They paused because of a report that the dog pack was coming their way. It was cold by now; Elvira and the Mountforts had blankets round their knees. Peter sat still for a few sec-onds after switching off the engine. His hand felt under the blanket, found and pressed her own.

That incident was enough to fill her mind as she dined two hours later with the manager of the resort and his wife. The manager talked fascinatingly about the reserve and his history, but Elvira was elsewhere. Peter was callous, unfeeling and she could not get him out of her mind. She knew that she was being thoroughly foolish, that even if the next two days produced something that could lead nowhere, that she owed Luis her loyalty, that she was verging on middle age and too old for such capers. It was not just Peter that she desired. Linked with him in a messy sort of way were the dead dinka, the bloody questions of the bush, reason or anarchy, neutrality or humanity, the Mountfort question about the purpose of all she had seen since she arrived. She felt dislocated, adrift from her moorings. She made poor conversational company.

'Is there anything more you'd like? Anything extra in your hut? I know they're a bit simple.'

Elvira moved even further from her moorings. 'Would it be possible for someone to bring me a newspaper? I'm a bit worried about my husband's business . . . he's having a tricky time . . .'

'Of course, Mrs de Brundt. I'll get your ranger to find one. He may have to go down to the shack by the airstrip. That's where we usually keep them. It'll only take him ten minutes. Let's see, Peter isn't it?'

She felt scared at her own success. But that did not prevent her undressing hurriedly and putting on night-dress and dressing gown. This was ludicrous, like a bad movie. But she produced a whisky bottle and two glasses from the fridge. The errand took Peter fifteen minutes. He had changed out of shorts into dark blue slacks with a white shirt open at the neck. He carried the *Johannesburg Star* and the *Financial Times*.

'How kind of you, Peter. I hope it wasn't a nuisance. Sit down and have a drink.'

He looked around, took in the dressing gown, the whisky, the turned-down bed.

'Does your fan need fixing?' His tone was brutal. In the roof of the hut the white metal fan moved slowly. Like everything in the reserve except her own good sense the fan was working perfectly.

'What do you mean? It's fine.'

'It's the phrase we use. Among the rangers.'

'For what?'

'Like khaki fever.'

'What on earth do you mean?'

'When clients want our night-time services.'

Peter sat down abruptly on the bed. Elvira was appalled – at his harsh manner, at her own absurd situation. The movie was getting worse and worse. One part of her insisted that he must be told to leave at once. The other wanted to fling herself at him and drag him down from the position of advantage he had taken. She hesitated.

'I have a girlfriend in Durban,' said Peter, still harsh. 'You asked earlier, that is the answer. I touched your hand because I had been rude.'

'Not rude at all, just private.' With a huge effort she mastered herself. 'Stay there. Please don't go.'

She went into the bathroom. She imagined him thinking she would come out without night-dress and dressing gown. Instead she tightened the dressing gown cord, and carefully washed all the make-up off her face. 'Forty, looking fifty,' she observed to the mirror.

'Can we talk about the animals?' she said, coming out. He sat on the edge of the bed, wary, his senses alert, like the antelopes they had seen that afternoon. But he sipped the whisky she poured.

'Mrs de Brundt . . .'

'Elvira.'

'Elvira, we are both tired, and unlike you I have work to do preparing for tomorrow morning. Tomorrow at five-thirty.'

'Before I let you go, do you believe that it's all ordered and right out there in the bush? We could have saved an antelope yesterday when we were with John.'

'Dinka.'

'Dinka. We didn't. To my mind we put ourselves at a level with the rest of the bush. But we're not. We're apart, we're human, we have an instinct to save life, to do good . . .'

She faltered. She had made her point. It sounded feeble but she felt it. When he stood up they faced each other, neither sure what would happen next. The disagreement and the sexual tension were mixed up together.

'The lions roaring after their prey,' Peter said slowly and unexpectedly.

'What lions?'

'My father used to take us to church in Bulawayo. Every Sunday, scrubbed spotless. Till my voice broke I was in the choir; we sang the psalms. ". . . The lions roaring after their prey do seek their meat from God . . . Thence all wait upon thee: that thou mayest give them meat in due season." That is the order of things. We are part of that order. It is not for us to upset it.'

'Even if the result is cruel, bloody, awful . . .'

'Even so.'

Elvira gathered her strength. She had tightened the dressing gown cord, stripped off the make-up. It was time for the final step.

'It would be best if I went with another ranger tomorrow.'

She still half hoped that he would hesitate at this closing of the door between them.

'You're probably right,' he said at once.

'Goodnight. And please think you may be mistaken.'

'Goodnight.'

So the next day, the last day, it was John again, also a young English couple. It was the first day for the English, so John had to begin his painstaking explanations over again. The English had plenty of questions, which suited Elvira. She felt suspended between the foolishness of yesterday and the reality of tomorrow. Luis would collect her and they would go back to the routines of their life, domestic comfort and boredom at Sandton, business worries in downtown Johannesburg. Today was a nothing day. The sun rose, blazed, sank.

They turned for home soon after the tracker turned on the searchlight. Elvira thought of suitcase and tips. The trackers obviously, Peter obviously not: but what about John? She had no idea what was suitable, and there had been no helpful little note of advice on the dressing table in the hut.

'Something rather exceptional is happening,' said John in his careful way, taking the radio from his ear. He did not explain or ask whether they wanted to change their homeward plans. After a word with the tracker he quickly reversed the Land Rover, drove back along the track for a mile, then headed abruptly into the bush.

'What's the drama?' asked Elvira, irritated.

'We're nearly there.'

'There' was a dried-up river, and the Land Rover driven by Peter. Along the river bed trotted a rhinoceros, behind the rhinoceros its baby, making a big effort to keep up.

'About three weeks old,' said John.

But that was not the drama. Wild dogs were the drama, about six of them. It was difficult to count as they swerved in and out of the lights. Two wild dogs trotted alongside the baby rhino, darting at it but not biting, trying to cut it off from its mother. It looked as if this had been going on for some time; the baby rhino was showing signs of distress. Its mother stopped at a point where the river bed widened and turned to confront the pack. The baby scurried to safety under her flanks. But the dogs multiplied round her, circling in and out of the shadows, long ears alert, silent and formidable, keeping well clear of the huge head and horn. The rangers turned off their engines. The rhino surveyed her enemies, then turned and began to lumber once again down the river bed. The Land Rovers restarted and moved in parallel through the bush, keeping their lights trained on the animals.

After three minutes the rhino paused again, took stock, changed tactics. She turned aside from the river bed and began to move into the gap of only twenty yards between the two Land Rovers driven by John and by Peter. She seemed to calculate that the wild dogs might be put off from following by the lights and the engine noise. She passed without hesitating through the gap. But something had failed in the communication between mother and baby. The baby hesitated before following her mother. The increased distance between them gave the two leading dogs their chance. They raced ahead of the baby, and cut it off from its mother. None of the animals showed the least awareness of the Land Rovers. The confrontation occurred within a yard of Elvira. The cudgel stored beneath the back seat was part of the vehicle's standard equipment. Without thinking Elvira grabbed it and swung at the leading dog just as it prepared to spring at the baby rhino. The dog aborted its spring and for the first time took notice of a human presence. His revolting smell filled Elvira with hatred and fear. She raised the cudgel again, though he was just beyond her reach. The movement decided the dog to attack this interference before returning to the baby rhino. It crouched to spring at Elvira, eyes fastened on the target. John in front seized his rifle. Elvira was puzzled that he managed to fire before the rifle reached his shoulder. The dog snarled for the first and last time, rolled over, kicked, died. Then Elvira saw Peter, out on his feet in the gap between the vehicles, rifle in hand, hair flopping over his forehead. The second dog fled back into the darkness, the baby rhino hurried forward to safety. Elvira knew that she was about to faint. She stayed conscious long enough to hear the charge of the mother rhino, to scream as Peter took the impact, to see him under the beast, then stretched, a crumpled heap of shirt and shorts, on the floor of the bush.

'He'll live,' said Luis, comforting her as she lay in bed in the hut. 'The horn missed him.'

'But if the horn missed him . . .'

'Her foot crushed his left rib into his lung. They've managed to stop the internal bleeding, so he's no longer in danger.'

'Can I see him?'

'They're going to keep him unconscious for several days yet. Otherwise the pain would be too great.'

Elvira kept asking questions so that she did not have to feel anything.

'Can they operate?'

'No. They rely on the lung to get rid of the bits of bone and heal itself. He'll be out of action for several months. But he should count his blessings.'

'Good morning, Mrs de Brundt.' She realised that John was in the hut too, hanging back while she talked to her husband. 'You had a fearful shock. I hope you're feeling better.'

'Yes, indeed.' Elvira chose words carefully. Her head ached, slowing down thought. 'Peter saved my life.'

'He was quicker with his rifle than I was. You were certainly in danger.'

'Of my life?'

'Not your life probably. But the dog might have clawed you. There would have been danger of infection.'

Careful, accurate John. But there was something else.

'There's something else which isn't right.'

She wished her mind would move faster. She had to think of it while John was still there. Luis wouldn't understand. She found it.

Peter was out of the vehicle. She confirmed to collect the thought. 'He was out of his Land Rover before I was in any danger.'

'Yes, Mrs de Brundt. I was surprised.'

'Why surprised?' asked Luis.

'Because it is our rule not to intervene except to save human life. Peter intervened before that moment was reached.'

'Luckily,' said Luis, not understanding.

'Luckily perhaps, though I would have shot the dog in time with my rifle.'

Elvira had reached the point.

'Peter intervened to save that baby rhino.'

'It seems so.'

John could not conceal his disappointment.

Elvira allowed herself a last recall of standing at the foot of the bed with Peter, where the two men stood now, of his argument and of hers. So after all she had won.

'I'm feeling better now. I think I'll get up and pack.'

6
FOG OF PEACE

They had ordered lunch to be served on the seven-seater jet because the Secretary of State would arrive too late for the official meal at Dublin Castle. The RAF lunch did not vary. The half-grapefruit sheltered at its heart a scarlet cherry. The seafood salad was abundant, and came with salad dressing in little plastic packets hard to open. A gâteau lush with cream lurked in the tiny stewards' pantry between the passenger cabin and the two pilots; but there would hardly be time for pudding on so short a flight. The Chablis was satisfactorily cold and of a different quality from the food.

The Secretary of State took a second glass of wine and looked through gaps in the clouds at grey-green fields and hills below, first of England, then of Wales. He enjoyed travel, even cooped up in the tiny HS125. He liked being with his team from the Northern Ireland Office – his Private Secretary, tall and scowling with anxiety, opposite him across the seafood salad, his curly-haired Chief Information Officer, a grizzled senior official on the aisle opposite, his protection officer up front. Two secretaries towards the rear gossiped about office dramas past and future, one with a Belfast voice which lilted more emphatically as the stories multiplied.

His brief lay open on his lap. He did not need to read it, though he could feel his Private Secretary willing him to do so. The young man was new, and meticulous. He would learn. The Secretary of State had spent most of the last few weeks on these negotiations and the whole of the morning at 10 Downing Street discussing the latest tactics. He could have written the brief himself. Anyway it was out of date. The Prime Minister that morning had insisted on a tougher variation. They had intelligence of two Blowpipe missiles smuggled by the IRA out of the Shorts factory in Belfast – a new threat that had to be countered. The Foreign Secretary, the Home Secretary, and he himself had quickly concurred. They decided not to agree to separate referendums North and South of the Border until the Provisional IRA had handed over all weapons above the calibre of a rifle. They then spent too long re-drafting the communique. Technical drafting points were already being discussed between the Irish and British delegates in Dublin Castle, but he would descend from the skies neatly in time for the main session in the early afternoon.

He did not know whether the Irish Government would accept this new precondition. Probably not today, though they would come round later. The Taoiseach was keen to hold these referendums as soon as possible, well before the Irish Parliamentary elections expected in the autumn.

The Secretary of State did not intend to linger in Dublin.

'You told them at Hillsborough I'd still be there in time for dinner?'

James, the Private Secretary, uncoiled his legs.

'Yes, Secretary of State. Your guests are invited for eight. I suppose we might be a bit late.'

'Not if I can help it.'

This was a dinner for personal friends. It was surprising how quickly it was possible to make such friends in Northern Ireland. And of course they liked coming to Hillsborough Castle, as did he. It wasn't really a castle but a large country house, comfortable, with good books, open fires, dark handsome pictures by Lavery, limes and beeches taller than their English counterparts, his welcoming wife, and David the butler with a tray of gin and whisky.

'Not if I can help it,' he repeated.

'Getting quite thick, sir,' said the protection officer in front of them.

They must be over the Irish Sea, but there was no sea in sight. A thick curling fog rose towards them though they had not yet begun their descent to Dublin. Sunlight caught the grey wing of the plane, then disappeared, as if for good. The fog reached up and engulfed them.

The steward appeared. Even though the HS125 was tiny, he used the same formality as if it were a VC10.

'The pilot's compliments, sir. The weather's closed in. We can't get in to Dublin at present. We could go west to Cork, or north to Aldergrove . . . or,' he hesitated, 'back to Northolt.'

'Damn,' said the Secretary of State.

'Shit,' said James, the Private Secretary, simultaneously and surprisingly, for up to then his vocabulary had been notably decorous. They looked at their watches. In Dublin Castle the lunch would begin in five minutes.

No problem about that. Denis Flack, Deputy Under-Secretary, could take his place as he had already done in the morning's preliminary talks. But Flack could not handle the main session beginning at 3 p.m. Flack did not know how the session at Number 10 had gone that morning.

'What happens if we circle above Dublin till it lifts?'

'We can do that, sir,' said the steward. 'We've enough fuel to try that for an hour or so. Fair chance of it lifting by then.' He sounded dubious.

It was as if they had entered a timeless zone. Nothing to show where they were or what was happening in the rest of the world. Neither light nor dark, neither fast nor slow, heading neither north, south, east nor west, just round and round in greyness that might be eternal. The Secretary of State was quite comfortable, and among a team who were friends. The girls continued to gossip till the gossip turned to giggles. The gâteau appeared, and imposed five minutes' silence until it had disappeared. The Secretary of State, declining gâteau, took a third glass of Chablis. James the Private Secretary fretted, making little notes for his master, fiddling with his watch, going forward with stooped head to confer with the pilot.

It seemed endless, but eventually they were down. Armoured cars ringed the runway, but this was routine. The reception was efficient. A helicopter flew them over Georgian squares to within the ramparts of Dublin Castle. A large and ancient Bentley drove them for two minutes from the helicopter pad into the main courtyard. The green copper dome of the Castle gleamed with wet. James looked at his watch for the umpteenth time. 'Ten past four exactly,' he said unnecessarily.

There was a gathering outside the main entrance, seething with the unmistakable motion of excited journalists. They could hear the click of cameras, the shout of photographers, and see their flashes in the dim afternoon light. The Taoiseach stood in the porch behind a battery of microphones. Flack, small, bald and somewhat flushed, was at his elbow. They could see that Flack was speaking, but he had stopped by the time the Secretary of State, moving very fast, had left the car.

'Sorry you were held up,' said the Taoiseach. 'We've done a good day's work.'

One journalist shouted a question to the Secretary of State, but was hustled away by Irish officials.

Under a dripping archway, apart from the Irish, Flack explained. Everything had gone very smoothly. Flack, though he did not say so, had enjoyed his brief hour of acting as a Minister.

The Irish had accepted all the British amendments to their draft. He had not heard that the Secretary of State was landing, only that he had been frustrated by the fog. There seemed no reason to hold things up. Indeed this might have wrecked the deal.

'And the arms proviso?'

'What arms proviso, Secretary of State?'

And of course Flack knew nothing of an arms proviso. It was not in his brief. It was not in the document he had signed. It was not in the agreement that the Taoiseach had just announced.

It was one of those moments of choice that come perhaps two or three times in a political career. The Secretary of State looked at Flack, at the Irish officials grouped a few yards away, at the dispersing journalists, at the Castle where Viceroys had held sway, where the prisoners of the Easter Rising had been held and shot. He thought of the Prime Minister, of the House of Commons, of his career. Even of his wife. Hard to do anything, hard to do nothing. Then he decided. To do nothing. To let it pass.

'Yes,' he said, approaching the Taoiseach. 'A good day's work. And now I deserve a drink.'

Twelve weeks later the Secretary of State approached Hillsborough by helicopter. The two referendums had gone smoothly. A low turn-out in the South and a predictable majority for a United Ireland; in the crucial referendum in the North a majority to maintain the Union with Great Britain. The constitutional parties had at once agreed the devolution plan that had been held in reserve for such an outcome. Sinn Fein had split. A minority had decided to continue the terrorist campaign. The main leaders were gathered with the other parties at Hillsborough to sign the agreement with the Secretary of State.

By the lake below the Castle three men waited under dripping beeches. They could just see the pad where the helicopter would land, though the weather was thickening. They wore the uniform of the Royal Ulster Constabulary, and were consulting the top secret itinerary of the Secretary of State's movements. Northolt, Londonderry, Coleraine, Antrim, Belfast, Hillsborough.

'A triumphal tour,' said one.

'Till the end,' said his companion.

The two Blowpipe missiles were at their feet. They were the ones stolen weeks earlier from the Shorts factory in

Belfast where they were manufactured. The Army helicopters had no countervailing techniques.

'Quiet, here he comes.'

They could hear the buzz of the two helicopters through the fog. They must be over the Maze prison, just a couple of miles away. Time to make ready the missiles.

The Sergeant addressed the Secretary of State on the intercom. He sat shivering in a borrowed Army greatcoat, earpads and safety belt in place. James was beside him, clutching a red box as if it were a precious child. It had already fallen once out of the helicopter into Ulster mud.

'Very sorry, sir, we can't get down. Fog particularly thick over your house. Danger of hitting the trees.'

The Secretary of State fiddled with his mouthpiece, 'So?'

'Aldergrove, I'm afraid, sir. A car will take you straight to Hillsborough. You'll be forty-five minutes late.'

'What's forty-five minutes in the history of Ireland?' asked the Secretary of State, but neither James nor the Sergeant replied.

Within two hours the agreement was signed, the champagne served, the Troubles ended. The lights of Hillsborough shone warmly out over the garden, the lake, the trees and the helicopter pad.

The two men from the dissident minority waiting by the lake had heard the cars drive up the other side of the house and guessed what had happened. They swore and, drawing their revolvers, scrambled up the garden slope towards the cars, desperate to retrieve something from the years of struggle even at the last minute. The RUC spotted them in their protective beams, closed in, scuffled, caught them.

The Blowpipes were discovered in the morning by a group of politicians strolling through the garden after breakfast, talking of constitutional matters, just as if the future of Ulster were theirs.

7
SEA LION

It wasn't working. It wouldn't work. This was his last week in the Islands. Perhaps one more conversation with the sea lions would do the trick.

Richard was allowed to use the motorbike on which old David Macgregor visited his sheep. He drove it brutally through the colony of penguins about half a mile from the knoll on which the farmhouse and hotel stood. A dirty cloud of their own droppings enveloped the birds as they waddled indignantly away. In his present mood the extraordinary tameness of the wild life was an affront to Richard's sense of reality. Why couldn't penguins and elephant seals and sea lions learn to protect themselves like ordinary creatures? Why couldn't David Macgregor and his like recognise that they lived next door to Argentina and thousands of miles from Scotland? But in both cases they didn't and wouldn't.

Richard made for the bluff at the end of the island and the memorial to HMS *Sheffield*. Somewhere out there, to the south of the most southerly of the Falklands, her tow line had finally snapped 14 years ago, and the work of the Exocet had been accomplished.

Richard could not afford to repay the publisher's advance, but knew he would have to. George Schonbrum could hardly reclaim the return air fare as well, but that was small consolation. It had seemed such a good idea over lunch at the Savoy, just the thing to revive his flagging reputation. Brilliant young historian turns the tables on his own Tory past and exposes the falseness of the Falklands War. Secrecy, of course, was essential. To Lady Thatcher, to the Foreign Office, to the Governor and to Mr Smith, the Curator of the Museum in Port Stanley, he had presented himself as working on a straightforward account of the war, updating the quick book put out at the time by Max Hastings and Simon Jenkins. They had all been most helpful. Richard had kept his good looks and could deploy plenty of boyish charm. Only Schonbrum the publisher knew that Richard had reached the answer before he started asking the questions.

Richard liked the company of the sea lions. They did not fuss like the penguins. They were not as gross or familiar as the elephant seals. They lay, a mix of tawny and black, on the rocks beneath him, economical with their movements and their grunts. There were eight of them on that particular stretch, more than usual, and looking along to the next bay Richard saw the reason. The French marine botanists were at it again, photographing through the glass bottom of their boat. They occupied all eight small white bedrooms of the hotel, which was why Richard was lodged with the farmer, David Macgregor. They were, he understood from Macgregor, making an immensely intellectual film, based on the ripples of the floating local seaweed or kelp, which they repeatedly photographed in all lights and all weathers.

Richard was one of those Englishmen who shuns the French for fear that they might be more intelligent than himself. He had made no contact with them. Macgregor had, however, told them with satisfaction the story of the young Frenchman who had mysteriously committed suicide on the island 40 years earlier. Macgregor's uncle had had to pull down a partition in the farmhouse to provide wood for his coffin. The four puny conifers struggling in David Macgregor's garden were still the only trees on the island. Though the Falklands were not as cold as Richard had expected, the wind was incessant.

Richard sat in the lee of a huge mound of tussock grass. Its roots were exposed by the wind, and he could see the black layer of ash from the time when the island had been on fire. The peat had burned for several months, set alight, it was supposed, by castaways in search of warmth. The Islands were full of such stories. Those of the 1982 war fitted well with the tales and emblems of earlier drama – skulls, masts, whalebones, the prows of abandoned vessels, and now the wreckage of crashed Mirages.

Richard heard the air taxi before he saw it approach the mown grass strip. The autumn light was fading and the Cessna did not linger. Within 10 minutes it was in the air again. A tall girl was carrying a suitcase to where David Macgregor was waiting in his Land Rover. Of course, his daughter Laura, back for Easter from Southampton University. 'She talks a bit,' David had said. Since David himself was monosyllabic, it was hard to say what the comment meant. David, a widower for 20 years, disliked any intrusion on his sheep and his solitude. Soon the airstrip would close for the winter, 'and there'll be an end to all this noise and pother,' David had remarked, as if he lived in Mayfair. Against this background Richard's evenings in the farmhouse had not sparkled. He had read and reread his research materials, but the answer to the Falklands problem lay dozing in front of the peat fire. There were no powers of force or charm that would turn David Macgregor into an Argentine citizen.

With Laura the evening was certainly different. She spoke at once as if they had met often before.

'How did you vote?' she asked.

Richard had forgotten it was election day in Britain.

'I voted by post. The ballot is secret.'

'Don't be tiresome. I need to know for my thesis on political communication. How did you vote?'

'I voted Labour for the first time.' Richard was 29. He spoke as if a lifetime of electoral experience weighed upon him.

Laura passed him the mint sauce. The lamb was home-bred. She had bought the mint sauce at Tesco's in Southampton on her way to the airport, together with the Cadbury's Fruit and Nut which her father particularly favoured. She was tall and freckled, too thin for Richard's taste, but with direct blue eyes which could not be ignored. As the evening passed and she moved about the kitchen and dining table in her tight jeans his first disappointment passed.

'How on earth did you turn Left? All those articles of yours belong to the sour Right.'

Richard wished she had mentioned the book rather than the articles. His biography of Sir Austen Chamberlain, published five years ago, had been well researched, well received, earned little. But it had opened the columns of the Right-wing press to him, editors paid well and Richard found he could earn more from bitter topical articles than from attempting another book. The more caustic the article, the higher the fee paid on behalf of Messrs Murdoch and Black. He carried a folder of recent articles in his suitcase to reassure him as necessary of his own cleverness.

'The Government is so awful,' he answered her question lamely. 'Anything would be better.'

'Then why did you try so hard to get selected for places like South Hants?'

'How the hell do you know that?'

She refilled his Nescafé.

'I told you. I am reading politics. I follow these things.'

She was getting warm. That had been the most humiliating year of his life. Handsome young historian, darling of *The Spectator*, constantly compared to the slashing early Disraeli – full of his own future, he had trailed round constituency selection committees being rejected by old women, estate agents and seedy councillors. He had conceived a fierce hatred of the present Conservative Party which neglected such obvious talent.

'That's all over now. I'm working on another book.'

David Macgregor had mumbled his way upstairs to bed. Outside the wind, never still, was rising and rattling the windows.

'You could cheat on the book, I suppose. I mean, you could decide after all that the Argentines offered us a good deal and Margaret Thatcher insisted on war to fix the '83 election.'

He stared at her again. His years as a columnist had taught him not to blush.

103

'I've given up wondering how you know what you know,' he said after a pause. 'It must be the second sight of the Macgregors.'

'It's John Wilson at the Museum in Stanley. He rang me in England to say you'd been nosing around the archives. Asking slanted questions. Trying to suggest that we were an unreasonable bunch. Or else a lot of fools exploited by electioneering politicians at home.'

'But it won't work!' Richard found himself saying to the girl what he had said to the sea lions.

Despite all those tendentious column-inches, he had started as a scholar and still believed in evidence. There were therefore still limits to what he could write. Unfortunately there was no evidence in London, or New York, or Buenos Aires or Stanley to support the thesis which he and Schonbrum had tossed around over lunch at the Savoy.

'I'm glad,' she said. Reaching out, she touched his hand. 'It would have been bad if you had come out against the Islands.' She paused. 'Maybe we can do you a good turn one day.'

'You have already,' he said, lightening the tone. 'The lamb was delicious, and . . .'

But she was already up the stairs.

The next morning he had time before the Cessna came for him. He went with Laura to see the Slipway. The wind was still stiff. Yesterday's clouds had blown away, and the waves sparkled as they formed, rose high and toppled in white explosion upon the rocks. The Frenchmen had wisely pulled their boat ashore. There was no harbour on Sea Lion Island. Before the days of the air taxi, supplies came to the farm three times a year and were hauled almost vertically on an iron pulley up a wooden slipway to a ledge of tussock grass 40 feet above deep water. The crew would scramble up the rocks to help David Macgregor and his father before him to work the pulley.

'Grief, look at that!'

Laura had reached the ledge first. Below them, exactly where the lighters had once bobbed and scraped against the rock face, was a smart white launch tossing furiously but tied to a rusty iron ring set in the rocks. It was empty.

'The French must have brought in a second boat.'

'No, look at that.'

Because of the lie of the land they now saw for the first time the cruise ship out in the bay which formed the southern shore of the island. In the sun it, too, shone white, and through her binoculars Laura could see the Greek flag.

'Greek, Russian, Japanese – they come quite often nowadays, but usually only to Stanley.'

Richard heard the footsteps before she did. 'Down,' he whispered loudly, pulling hard at her sweater. They lay side by side on the ledge, concealed by the long wiry hummocks of grass from the upward path which sailors had once made and which the sheep preserved. A young man, dark and wiry, was near the top. He carried a hand-held TV camera. Behind him followed a girl, looking exactly like him, carrying what seemed to be a canvas gun-case slung over her shoulder.

Long ago sailors had built a small cairn to mark the top of the Slipway. The couple paused at the cairn, and spoke together. They were too far off for Richard to know more than that they were speaking a language he did not understand. The young man began to organise his camera. The girl opened the long tubular canvas case and took out the contents. A couple of neat movements and she had achieved her purpose. The camera made it immortal.

'Grief!' said Laura again.

'*Bellissimo*,' shouted the young cameraman.

On the day when the new British Government was formed, the blue and white flag of Argentina, rooted in the cairn, flew bravely over the southernmost of the Falklands.

Without a word or gesture to Richard, Laura charged across the open space straight at the flag. She shoved the amazed girl aside, snatched the flag, and threw it down the Slipway. Without any concern for her own safety, she watched it rattle down between the parallel ridges of wood into the sea, and spread lazily in the waves. When she turned round she faced the young man's pistol.

'That was not an intelligent action,' he said in excellent English. But that was all. Afterwards Richard often asked himself why he had acted as he did. No calculation, no thought, just an impulse which changed for ever his view of himself.

Richard was in reasonable training. Vague memories of the rugby field produced the perfect tackle.

'It wasn't loaded,' he said, picking up the gun. The Argentine sat on the grass, nursing his knee.

'Of course not. We are not bandits.'

'At least we have the picture,' said his sister, 'which is what we came for.'

The young man got up. 'Permit me to introduce ourselves. We are Roberto and Susanna Tuzman, partners in the public relations company of that name, based in Buenos Aires.' He broke off, and in a different tone shouted at Laura: 'Stop that! It is not yours.' But Laura had already thrown the camera down the Slipway. Its descent was noisier than that of the flag, and ended dramatically with a combination of crash and splash.

'Better go while you can,' said Richard. 'I don't suppose the Greeks will wait for ever.'

The two invaders took his advice.

'It would be better if you did not mention this to anyone,' said Roberto Tuzman.

'*Viva las Malvinas*,' said his sister.

Then they were down the path, and three minutes later the launch was on its way.

Laura gave him a kiss just before he boarded the Cessna. But that was that. No shared comradeship after victory, no discussion of what had happened or why.

'Not much point,' was all she said when he began. 'It's all pretty obvious. A PR stunt which went wrong. Lucky we were there. I've sent a radio message to Stanley with the gist of it.'

Richard never knew what that message of hers contained. The Cessna came down at Mount Pleasant, and Richard was put without explanation into an Army helicopter. Within 10 minutes he landed on the grass between Government House and the elegant new Comprehensive School.

The Governor was there, with his red London taxi, also the Commander British Forces, Mr Smith, the Curator of the Museum, elected Councillors and the Chief Executive. Four police officers saluted. A television camera flashed.

'You didn't give us time to get the Marine band organised,' said the General.

'Stout work,' said the Governor. 'You'll stay overnight

with Hilda and myself, I hope. A lot of people will want to hear from you direct.'

The next 24 hours were a splendid muddle. John Major had been re-elected with a majority of 20. The British press linked this with the repulse of a second Argentine invasion of the Falklands. Lady Thatcher sent Richard a telegram. He broadcast repeatedly. He held a public meeting in the hall at Stanley, attended by a high proportion of the town's inhabitants. He tried to get in touch with Laura, but in vain. He ate a huge celebratory lunch with much Chilean wine at the Upland Goose Hotel. He had a few minutes of final packing before he left in the Governor's red taxi for the airport.

He would never see Laura again, and would hardly think of her. But he remembered what she had said about the Islands doing him a good turn. He thought of that rugby tackle on Sea Lion Island. He took out of a drawer his research material and first notes for his book 'The Falklands Falsehood', together with a folder of his recent press articles.

Slowly but without regret he tore them up and dropped them in the crested wastepaper basket of the spare bed-room at Government House.

8

HELTER SKELTER

It was the rule of the villa that the largest and oldest faded pink umbrella was allocated to the Duchess. One of Angelo's first duties each morning was to slot it into its pedestal under the olive tree at the edge of the clearing, where her elder son had built the swimming pool. From this vantage point the Duchess commanded a full view of all poolside activity. The house itself, skilfully scooped out of the mountainside, stood at the top of two miles of steep winding drive. The tennis court and the swimming pool both required a further climb, seven minutes for fit 30-year-olds, up steps lined with pink and white oleanders. The Duchess rarely visited the tennis court, but each day for three weeks in August, unless the weather had broken, she took 15 minutes to climb to the pool.

Below in the valley the clock of San Leonardo in Compito began to strike 12. On the eleventh note of San Leonardo the clock of San Ginese in Marinaia, visible on the next spur of hills, took up the message. This was normally the best time of the day. The heat was already strong enough to work its trick of wrapping each human being in a cloak of solitude. Life had slowed down. Only the cicadas competed in noisy activity.

No one was in the pool, and the Duchess surveyed the four figures reclining beside it. Her eye found first the cause of her present strong discontent. So strong indeed that she had almost decided on a headache, which would keep her in the total shade down below on the terrace. There her husband and the elderly novelist Francis Litherland spent their mornings, the Duke snoozing over a thriller, the novelist scribbling, in an exercise book, glass on table. She had exerted herself up the steps in the cause of duty, only to find her discontent massively increased. For the girl, Linda, was sunbathing topless. Her generous breasts showed by their colour that this was the rule rather than the exception. Her golden hair was arranged in long ringlets spread decoratively over the dark blue towel on which she lay.

The Duchess, an honest woman, had to admit that this was not the first time a girl had shed her top round the pool at La Freddiana. Alexander, the child of her middle age, was dear to the Duchess, but his taste in girls had certainly deteriorated in the past three years. Alexander had picked this latest brassy specimen off some boat at Porto Ercole, and brought her at once to his brother's villa, even though he had already invited a guest for that week in the form of his pleasant friend Nicholas. Last night, being her first at La Freddiana, Linda Pallett had drunk too much, argued loudly about matters of which she knew nothing, and been offensive in turn to everyone in the room. She had even called the Duke useless, not once but several times. It had been an interminable evening. Alexander had defended her for an hour or so, then fallen silent, and finally marched her out saying, 'Goodnight all. I know how to put a stop to this.'

The girl was quiet enough now, soaking in the sun, not snuggling close either to her elder son or to the Grevilles at the far end of the pool. Of Alexander there was no sign, though yesterday the two had been inseparable.

Of course it was the Prime Minister's visit that made the difference. The Duchess was not narrow-minded. A blonde of Alexander's could pass through La Freddiana, argumentative and slightly drunk, without leaving permanent harm behind her. The disaster lay in the coincidence. Up to now the Prime Minister's arrival tomorrow had been worried about in terms of ordering a better wine than the villa itself produced, testing and retesting the relevant bathroom and lavatory, scrubbing the window seat cushion where, years ago, Alexander had spilt Coca-Cola. But of what use was good wine and safe plumbing with Linda Pallett in the house? She would certainly, on last night's form, attack the Prime Minister at all points. And yet so much hung on the night and two days which the Prime Minister was to spend with them.

The Duchess felt the need to break out of the zone of solitude created by the heat and communicate with her elder son.

'Thomas,' she called.

Her son at once left the shelter of his umbrella by the pool and came towards her, as if glad to be relieved of the tedium of his own company.

'Filthy,' said Alexander Ruthven, kicking a crumpled cigarette packet. 'Why have the Italians become such pigs?'

'Why are you in such a ludicrous temper?'

113

They sat on the edge of a rampart on the walls of Lucca, legs dangling like schoolboys. In fact the occasional litter and dog mess did not spoil the general pleasantness. The old city of Lucca stayed agreeably contained within its pink walls, crowned by an avenue of plane trees. To the north the hills grew hazy in the heat. Below them small boys kicked a football in the green meadows between the walls and the roaring ring road.

They had been turned out of the Duomo because Alexander's shorts were too short. Over the years his shorts had grown shorter and his hair longer, whereas in both respects Nicholas remained the same. As undergraduates at the same Oxford College, they had more than once travelled Europe together, sometimes with girls, sometimes not, trying not to lose their Euro-rail passes, making no plans, educating themselves despite themselves. Then their paths separated. It was far from clear why after this gap in friendship Alexander had asked Nicholas out of the blue to spend a week at La Freddiana.

At 24 Alexander still dressed like a messy 18, and this was an error. His shorts cut into his thighs, his fair hair was bound into a pigtail at the back, his chin showed signs of doubling.

'You didn't shave this morning.'

'I hate that bloody girl.'

'You swept her off last night as if you loved and owned her.'

'She insulted everyone round the table, one by one, even Dukey. Then she insulted me in private.'

'I don't ask for the details.'

'You'd have had them once, without asking.'

So, for a moment, Alexander recognised the distance which had grown between them.

'Shall we go?' Nicholas stood up. They had failed to view the Cathedral, had bought the English newspapers, and ordered a fish for the Prime Minister's lunch the next day. There was no further reason to stay in Lucca.

As they walked to find Alexander's battered BMW, Nicholas reflected that he owed something more to people who had been kind to him over many years.

'Don't forget the Prime Minister is coming tomorrow.'

'Hence the fish. How could I forget?'

'Hence the need for some restraint.'

Alexander laughed. 'After all these years you get me so wrong. The Dutch is mad to suppose she'll get Tom promoted by inviting the PM to savour the Ruthven charm in its summer habitat. But behind the scruff and the sex I'm a high Tory, and always will be. Once the PM's in the house my mouth is shut, and so is my bedroom door.'

Francis Litherland, veteran of letters, looked across the terrace to the sleeping form of the Duke of Stirling. If the two young men had asked him to go with them to Lucca, he would have accepted. It was galling that everyone should assume that he, like the Duke, had geriatric tastes. He had no intention of climbing the steps to the swimming pool, having some time ago lost any relish in taking off his own clothes or seeing women largely without theirs. In his view swimming pools and tennis courts were enemies of civilisation. Francis Litherland had masked his disappointment by claiming to have much work to do, and indeed three novels stood on the ornate white iron table beside him, ripe for reviewing. But he found it difficult to read or write, and the sight of the snoozing Duke a few yards away added to his irritation.

What an ass the man had been the night before, failing in his first duty of protecting his guests from attack. That slut Linda should never have been allowed in the house. She had found a copy of his poems in Alexander's room and had brought it down to dinner, having marked passages which she read out with mockery over the coffee. Twenty years ago, when Francis had taught Tom and signed that book for the Duchess, his tastes and his style had been more florid. That poem which she had singled out about Greek athletes preparing for contest, for example – he would not have written it now.

The Duchess and Tom had proved quite inadequate in turning the talk, and the Duke, flushed and incoherent, had intervened only with some obscure reminiscence about his fairground experiences as a boy in Scotland. Who had said that a Lowland Duke was the lowest form of intellectual life? This one was degenerating fast. How to get rid of the slut? He resolved to speak to the Duchess at lunch and not to take no for an answer.

'*Have* you asked her to go?'

The Duchess shifted her chair a little so that her elder son, now sitting beside her, could have some shade. By that hour the olive was already ineffective.

'She's going on Friday anyway. Alex is taking her to Pisa airport.'

They both knew this was a feeble reply to give on Tuesday, with the Prime Minister coming tomorrow.

But Tom went on. 'I wish you hadn't asked the PM here at all. I promise you it will make no difference.'

'It's your house, Tom, not mine. You asked her. Whether it works will depend on what impression we all give.'

Neither wanted to pursue the argument. It was hot, and they were allies. The Duchess gazed down with affectionate irritation at the bald spot on her son's head. That bald spot signified five years as a Parliamentary Under Secretary, first at Energy, now at Health, the junior form of Ministerial life. Tom had worked hard, made no mistakes, remained wholly loyal and received no promotion. He had renounced his father's title, so that could not be the problem. Indeed, the Duchess knew there was no problem, because by now she would have ferreted it out if it existed. A newspaper had written that her son was dull. The Duchess had admitted to herself the grain of truth in the remark. Tom was not really dull. On a good day, when he got his nose out of his official paper, he could talk well, think imaginatively and make his friends laugh, including Italians in their own language. Privately she saw Tom as No. 2 in the Foreign Office, but only if he put his wares in the window.

'Get Alex to persuade her to go.'

'But he wants to bed her.'

Tom knew his mother was not prudish and was surprised at her strong reaction.

'Don't be vulgar. Anyway he's left her here this morning. That's hardly devoted.'

'Only because he's in a sulk. He'll be buzzing around the hive again by evening.'

'Then it'll have to be you, Tom. You must tell her at lunch that she's got to pack.'

The Grevilles were known to the world and to each other as highly organised. They had no children, and the organisation of their finances, their pleasures and their occasional good works took up the whole of their time. In August, they were usually invited to La Freddiana for a week – the Ruthvens banked at Grevilles – and they always accepted. At La Freddiana, they swam, slept and ate, contributed moderately to the conversation, and generously to the tip for Lena and Angelo at the end of the week. Their lives were so evenly conducted that any disturbance, however mild, affecting one partner was noticed by the other.

'It was almost as if she knew you,' said Leonora. They shared an umbrella by the deep end of the pool. 'She gave you a sinister smirk.'

Julian Greville was uncharacteristically cross. 'She was a secretary in the City. I can't be expected to remember every secretary I bump into in a lift.'

'There are bumps and bumps. So you do remember her.'

'The face is vaguely familiar. The bosoms I never saw until today. I'm pretty sure she never worked at Grevilles.'

Leonora had to be content with that.

The object of this attention lay face down in the full sun, her back shining with cocoa butter. From time to time she propped herself on her elbows to read *Cosmopolitan*, and to show the Grevilles, Tom and the Duchess what she was made of.

Ignoring this provocation, the Duchess moved down the agenda.

'I wanted a word about your father.' Tom sat still.

'You saw how he was last night,' the Duchess continued. 'An hour of silence, then he weighed in with a wholly irrelevant story about the Kelso Fair in his boyhood. Sitting on a mat, hurtling down round and round a tower, shooting out rather scared at the bottom, still going at a great rate. He took me once and I cried. It had all gone by the time Alex arrived.'

'Just as well. It was definitely dangerous. Helter Skelter it was called. I think I signed a Liberal petition against it.'

'But there was more to it than that yesterday. I'm worried about him.'

'Dukey looks well.'

'He hates being called Dukey. Yes, he always complains about coming here, and thrives once he's arrived. But yesterday afternoon . . .'

For some reason the Duchess decided not to end the sentence. Afterwards she regretted this.

Lunch, on which much dramatic expectation had been fixed, proved an anticlimax. Not in the culinary sense, for Lena had tested as main course the pasta which she intended as a preliminary for dinner with the Prime Minister the next evening. An outer ring of zucchini enclosed the rice which in turn enclosed the special 'sugo' devised by Lena's Venetian grandmother.

This completed the colours of the national tricolour and put everyone in a slightly exalted mood. Alex sat next to Linda, though whether as her protector or her jailer was not clear, for he said little, and ate largely.

Grapes and peaches and cheese, the local white wine in a yellow bottle without label, and the fizzy mineral water circulated steadily. The gaps between spoken words became longer, until the cicadas made most of the conversation. The sun filtering through the thick leaves of the trellised vine had a soporific effect. Then Linda stood up. She had put a pink wrap over her pink and green bikini, and wore huge dark glasses with a pink frame despite the shade of the vine.

'I would like to make a short announcement. I have been invited to stay here until Friday, and until Friday I shall stay. Only the Carabinieri could move me, and I doubt if they could get up the sodding drive. So, Your Graces, my Lord, Ladies and Gentlemen, you are stuck with me, and I shall now take my siesta.'

Because La Freddiana was built into a vertical hillside, the main bedrooms were at the same level as the terrace where they lunched, the sitting room and a lesser terrace being below. They could hear the clack of the girl's heels along the corridor, then the loud slam of her bedroom door.

Alex put his head in his hands and stared at his peach stones. The Duchess considered whether the necessary action should be concerted among those present, and decided not. Tom had told his mother that he intended to speak to Linda over the coffee, drawing her aside from the others. Linda had outwitted him by taking no coffee.

'A thoroughly vulgar girl,' she said, dismissing the subject and ending the meal.

Nicholas lay on his bed in his swimming trunks reading an Agatha Christie. He had schooled himself against the siesta, and so captured two hours for light reading. Heavy reading in the form of his law books lay around him, but between three and five he felt absolved from them. What an amazing flow of books that amiable Mrs Christie had produced. She was at her best when describing a small, closed world of people thrown together, say in a train or a hotel, without knowing each other well. Out of the ordinary, when subjected to pressure, sprang the extraordinary. Take La Freddiana for example . . .

He was prevented from dozing by the sound of Alex swearing and kicking at a locked door. It was a tedious sound, and there were no prizes for guessing which door and why. Within a minute of the rebuff Alex was with him. He threw himself into a chair by the open window.

'There's never been a lock on that bloody door. There are no locks on any doors in this bloody house, not even the downstairs loo.'

'Were you thrown out or did you never get in?'

'She must have begged a key from Lena. I didn't know they existed.'

'Scrap her, Alex.' Nicholas closed his book. 'Whatever happens this week, you will have forgotten her by Christmas.'

'What d'you think I am?' Alexander came and stood over Nicholas, hand on hips. 'D'you think I'm one of those bums who serves at bars along the coast, picking up a different girl each week from under the ombrellini?'

In his unbuttoned faded shirt and tight shorts, grubby fair hair now loose around his neck, that was exactly what Alex did look like.

'The trouble with you, Nicholas, is you're just passive, a spectator, a voyeur. You never do anything. You're the only person in this house who's never achieved anything in his life. And at this rate never will. Have you ever considered that?'

A good, strong exit line, followed by silence. The rest of the house was still, obedient to the siesta. After a few minutes' looking into himself, Nicholas also snoozed.

But the siesta at La Freddiana did not run its course. The inhabitants were disturbed by two different phenomena which occurred at about the same time, namely about

121

half-past four. Those, like Francis Litherland and the Grevilles, whose rooms looked up the hill to the rough scrub, were woken by an ominous crackling, and, so Francis added, by a pungent smell of burning which led to a rapid dream of Hieronymus Bosch and hellfire, causing him to leap from his bed, shouting for water.

Water was also the theme that indirectly disturbed those whose rooms looked on the terrace and the parking space. A truck containing a captain of Carabinieri with three other uniformed officers squealed round the final bend of the formidable drive. The Duchess, who never slept deeply, was on the doorstep before him, with Tom quickly at her shoulder. The Captain saluted. He was smart, young and enjoying himself.

'La Contessa Riffan?' he asked courteously. Stretching a point in the peerage, the Duchess agreed. Captain Ferretti began his tale in English, but turned to Italian with relief when he saw that both his audience understood.

The wind having changed, a forest fire, which had been confined to the uninhabited upper ridges of the mountain, was now moving down the slopes. Thanks to the untiring efforts of the *vigili da fuoco*, there was no immediate threat to the Countess or to her son or to their distinguished guests. But it was necessary to take the initiative against the fire during the hours of daylight, and for this reason it had been decided by the competent authorities to deploy helicopters. The two helicopters dedicated for this purpose carried, as the Countess and her honourable son perhaps knew, large canvas containers which they lowered into whatever suitable reservoirs of water were available, and then carried to the fire and unloaded on strategic points to extinguish the flames or check their advance.

It displeased him to tell them, but much the most convenient immediate reservoir for this purpose was the
swimming pool of La Freddiana. He therefore had been
instructed by his colonel in Lucca to present his compliments to the 'Riffan' family, and formally request the use of
their water, which the resources of the state would eventually replace. He apologised for the urgency of the
request, but – he spread his hands, and a cry of alarm from
Francis Litherland at the back of the house made his point
for him.

Tom and his mother did not need to consult. They knew
the form. In August, the helicopters of the firefighting
force, with their huge, red, dangling canvas bags, were a
familiar sight. The captain almost certainly had legal
powers if his polite request was refused. It was a disaster of
course at one level to lose the pool, with the Prime
Minister imminent, but it did not occur to either of them to
plead those grounds.

'Of course,' said the Duchess. The captain, sensing a
dramatic need, kissed her hand.

There followed three hours of memorable activity. La
Freddiana became the advance post of the struggle against
the fire. The plan was to hack a corridor through the
thick scrub along the false crest about half a mile above
the villa, wide enough to stop the flames. Two squads of
vigili worked with saws and axes to achieve this.
Alexander and Nicholas joined them, taking tools from
Angelo's shed. Linda, emerging to everyone's surprise in a
sensible shirt and old jeans, insisted on doing the same.
The noises of forestry joined with the continuing crackle
of the flames.

123

Particles of smoke began to speckle Lena's washing, hung discreetly between two olive trees on the unfashionable side of the kitchen. The Duke and Duchess established a bar on the terrace, although as the Duke said, it wasn't a real bar because the *vigili* only wanted water or Coca-Cola. They came down in ones and twos for a ten-minute break, and sat silent, hands round a glass, under the trellis. They were streaked with sweat and grime. The Duchess offered the use of the shower in her pink bathroom, but it was refused.

'Grazie, signora . . . forse piú tardi.'

The helicopter clattered deafeningly three times over the swimming pool, its rotors stirring up dust and agitating the olives. The Grevilles and Francis Litherland were on duty up there, but in fact the scarlet canvas bag was lowered, filled and raised without any help needed from the ground.

There was a moment of drama when Linda was sent back from the fire with a message for the headquarters in Lucca asking for the third standby squad to be sent at once. The helicopter radio had broken down. Linda swore foully when they found that the telephone, too, was out of order, no doubt because the line ran through the burnt area. She came out on the terrace and downed a glass of water.

'I'll take my car to Lucca with the message.'

'Or just go to the bar in the village. You can ring from there,' said Tom.

'Better idea,' said Linda.

'Go in Alex's car,' said Tom. 'It's faster.'

'No difference if I'm only going to the bar in San Leonardo. I'll take mine. Bye bye then.'

'Perhaps not too bad a girl after all,' said Tom, watching her dust.

'Don't be silly,' said the Duchess sharply. 'A crisis brings out the best in everyone. This is misleading. The best retreats again afterwards. People show their true nature in day to day life, not in emergencies.'

The third squad arrived within half an hour, though the party at the villa were slow to realise this as they took a more northerly track, directly to the fire and avoiding the village.

Soon the heat began to ebb from the day and the drama from the situation. The noise of axes and the crackle of the fire had stopped, and smoke no longer reached La Freddiana. The helicopter was no more to be seen.

At about seven, Alexander and Nicholas appeared at the pool, grunted an apology to Mrs Greville, stripped to underpants and lay still in the foot of water that remained.

'Over for the day?'

'The fire is out in this sector. Still going strong at the other edge, but moving away from us. No more to be done.'

Ten minutes later, Captain Ferretti of the Carabinieri appeared again at La Freddiana. He saluted smartly. His uniform had been near no fire. This time he was not enjoying himself.

'I came to thank you for your co-operation, which has been most generous . . .'

'It is nothing, Captain . . .' said Tom, about to propose hospitality.

But the captain had not paused.

'But I must tell you, sir, that there is a car off the track near the bottom of your *strada privata*.' They looked at each other.

'That must be . . .'

'In the car there is a girl. She is dead. Her neck has been broken. I think, when the car hit the tree.'

Francis Litherland dropped his glass on to the flagstone. The splinters scattered widely, reaching almost everyone in the group. The Coca-Cola ran red on the stones.

'This discussion is getting us nowhere. I will tell you what I have decided.' As her elder son spoke, the Duchess nodded approvingly from the sofa. At her feet a spiral coil burned slowly to ward off mosquitoes. Although it was past eleven, it was still very warm. They sat almost in darkness, just one lamp, with the windows open and a full moon calm beyond the stone pines. In the Duchess's experience, nature could be relied on for particular displays of tactless beauty at moments of difficulty. But she must concentrate on what Tom was saying. If only the Prime Minister were there she would see what he was made of.

'Of course we all hope that Linda's death was an accident . . .'

'Of course. Those hired cars are notorious.' Mrs Greville sat on a cushion at her husband's feet.

'Could you please not interrupt, Leonora. But the police clearly suspect foul play. That is why we have been politely told to stay here until they begin their questioning tomorrow. Nothing said in the past couple of hours obscures the fact that Linda was unpopular with everyone here.'

'You all hated her, I loved her,' said Alexander, clutching his knees.

His brother stared at him.

'That was a silly remark, second-rate and theatrical. So far as the rest of us were concerned, dislike is not the same

126

as hatred. The distinction is crucial when it comes to murder. As for you, the girl was more unpopular with you than with any of us, for a reason you know well.'

'She wouldn't go to bed with me.' Alexander grinned, and Nicholas realised that his earlier remark had been a tease.

'Precisely. Now it goes without saying that we shall all co-operate fully with the police tomorrow. For tonight, I am asking Nicholas to take a hand.'

Nicholas looked blank. 'I would say, Nicholas, that you were less set against Linda than anyone else. You have a cool mind. You know some Italian. I want you to look round her room. And I want anyone who has something to say in private to say it to Nicholas before the police come. It is just possible that as an Englishman who knows us well, Nicholas may be able to put something together which would escape the police. He might also prevent the police leaping to some absurd conclusion simply because we don't communicate with them adequately. Are you willing, Nicholas?'

'It's really your job.'

'I pass it to you. Willing?'

'Willing.'

'One thing puzzles me.' The Duke had ambled off to bed, still telling at large his story about the Helter Skelter at the Kelso Fair, and the others had soon followed his example. Nicholas was using his authority to search the dead girl's room. Thomas and his mother were left alone in the sitting room.

It was a room rarely used, because the way of life was outdoors. A spring had gone on the sofa at either end of which they sat. The huge bookcase beside them overflowed with the bric-a-brac of holidays – paperbacks, maps and guidebooks, jigsaw puzzles and Monopoly, a few elegant books on Tuscany presented by grateful guests.

'One thing puzzles me, Thomas. The girl went to send a message to get more firemen. She died before she sent the message. Yet the firemen came.'

'They managed to fix the helicopter radio after she left. They sent a second message that way.'

'You got hold of the PM?'

'I talked to Number Ten as soon as the phone was reconnected. They were very understanding. They'll get a message to her straight away.'

'Where is she tonight?'

'With Visentini, the textile man, near Milan. They thought she'd probably fly straight back to London from Milan tomorrow.'

'Sad.'

'We won't go over all that again.'

'Bed, I think.'

'Bed certainly.' They kissed. 'A bad day.'

'A bad day, Thomas. But pick ourselves up . . .'

'And dust ourselves down.'

'And be on our way.'

It had been a nursery saying.

After he had looked through Linda's room, Nicholas brushed his teeth before going to bed. He was far from clear what else Tom expected him to do. He had no authority or inclination to summon the inhabitants of the villa one by one. He judged that one or two might wish to say things to him which they would not want to put just like that to the police. There were English nuances that would not easily translate. But they would want to sleep on it and tackle him in the morning.

All except one, of course. Because the tap was running and he brushed his teeth with vigour, Nicholas did not hear the bedroom door open, but in the mirror he saw Alexander in the doorway. He turned.

'Come in.'

'I mean to.'

But there was no challenge in the voice. Alexander slumped on to the bed. He was exhausted, grey, collapsed. Because he had been less successful than Nicholas in washing the grime from his face and neck, he looked older.

'Two things. First, I don't kill little girls.'

'Has anyone suggested that you do?'

'Almost everyone looks at me as if I did.' He sat up. 'But the second is more important. This afternoon, after I left you and before the fire, I went and sat in the car. Her car. It was blazing hot. The leather scorched my skin.'

'Why on earth . . .'

'I wanted to think about her. Her small things were there . . . sun lotion, spare glasses, the map I drew her of how to get here . . . I thought it would be easier to think straight.'

'But?'

'But it wasn't. Just a hot blank. No way forward, no way back.'

'How long were you there?'

'Ten minutes, maybe more.'

Nicholas hesitated. 'Why do you tell me this?'

'To get it off my chest.'

'Only that?'

'Not only that. Lena saw me. She was carrying some washing into the laundry. I pretended not to see her.'

'But she certainly saw you.'

'I was not hiding. She saw me sitting at the wheel of Linda's car. And she will tell the police.'

'Alex, you used to be the world's worst mechanic. When we travelled together even I knew more about the inside of a motor car.'

'Still true.'

'That's the real puzzle,' said Nicholas. 'Almost everyone has a motive, and because of the siesta, no one, I suspect, has an alibi. But the motives aren't strong enough for the deed. And those who had the motive fall at the next fence of my powerful investigation.'

'Namely?'

'If the girl was murdered, it was by tampering with her car. But I have never in my life met a set of people so apparently incompetent in mechanical matters. I doubt if any one of you could change a light bulb.'

'Angelo changes the light bulbs. He always has.'

'Precisely.'

'I must go to bed.'

'Goodnight.'

'I'm glad I told you,' said Alexander.

'Goodnight.'

Nicholas, to get himself to sleep, picked up a book by Francis Litherland which he had found in the sitting room.

Nicholas took his peach and croissant and coffee across to a rickety garden table at the far end of the terrace from the table where breakfast was laid. It was eight o'clock, early by the standards of La Freddiana, and no one else, except

Lena, had yet appeared. Angelo was watering the petunias with a leisurely hose.

Francis Litherland emerged from the house, looked round, and came over. He wore an expensive purple silk shirt, two buttons undone and one missing, above cheap grey flannel trousers.

'You've set up a confessional, I see. But I was without sin towards the fearful Linda. I did not even lust after her in my heart.'

'You loathed her.'

'Loathed, loathed? On the basis of one evening's conversation I judged that she was an ignorant, arrogant slut. But that was a cool, objective judgement.'

'She was ruder to you than to anyone. That Greek athlete. You did not like it.'

'But, as Thomas said last night, dislike does not normally lead to murder. Nor do I have the faintest knowledge of the inside of a motor car.'

Nicholas paused. It was a critical moment.

'"The Mills of God."'

'"The Mills of God"?'

'Your novel. Published in 1960. It contains a detailed account of the hero working unsuccessfully in the car repair section of a garage in Brixton.'

'It was a subtle analogy with the human condition. How many of us look successfully under the bonnet of life?'

'It contained a mass of technical detail.'

'Researched at the time, at once forgotten. The artist has to clear out the attics of his mind. He has no room for clutter.'

'Quite so. Do you remember dedicating this copy to the Duke and Duchess?'

'It was years ago. I was still flattered by their acquaintance.'

'You dedicated it to my "two fellow mechanics".'

Another pause, then Francis laughed. 'Of course, you would not know. Mary served her country during the war in something called FANY. The Fanies drove immense trucks with great pride. The family album has several snaps of Mary supine under lorries. In dungarees, not attractive.'

'And the Duke?'

'Archie was a rally driver in his youth. Amateur, of course, it was a craze. He hit a wall eventually. The wall was small and suffered most, but he gave the sport up.'

'Oh God.'

'Have I not helped?'

'The reverse. You have shown me that three people whom I had ruled out all unexpectedly have, or had at one time, the knowledge necessary to fix a car and commit a murder.'

Francis smiled without fear.

'Time I got my coffee. It will not be nearly so tasty in prison.'

'So you found my cheque?'

'It was not difficult.'

Julian Greville was the next guest to breakfast alongside Nicholas's chair.

'She worked in our international division. She left her purse in the office one evening and came back to get it after the theatre. Just in time to eavesdrop on a delicate conversation with the Cayman Islands. Damn it, this was eight years ago. She's much older than she looks.'

'A long time ago,' said Nicholas, with some pity.

'I could still be prosecuted for fraud and sent to jail.'

'Has she asked for money before?'

'No, yesterday was the first time. That cheque you found was half of what she asked.'

'You are pleased that she cannot ask you again?'

'Yes of course . . .' He swerved. 'But not that way.'

Thoughtfully, before the man left him, Nicholas tore up Greville's personal cheque for £50,000.

Three hours later the sun had once again asserted power over Tuscany. Captain Ferretti and Nicholas sat opposite each other across the table under the pergola. It had been cleared of breakfast, but Ferretti had allowed himself to be persuaded into a glass of white wine. He was exhausted.

'So it was definitely murder?' asked Nicholas.

'Without doubt. The hydraulic brake pipe had been loosened. The brake fluid formed a pool which you may see on the gravel. It is amazing that she kept to the road as long as she did.'

They sat in silence, each nursing a glass.

'If you had all been Italian,' said Ferretti, 'I would still be tired and confused. But it would have been for the opposite reason.'

'Too much information.'

'Of course. Everyone would have told me everything about the girl, about the villa, about the afternoon, and it would have added up to far too much. The sheer abundance would have made nonsense.'

'Whereas?'

'Nothing. They are stiff. They do not enjoy the excitement. They do not excuse themselves or accuse others.'

'No one has an alibi. Not even me.'

'The siesta often has that effect. It is the bane of Italian criminology. Everyone is separated and ostensibly asleep. When the crime is committed during the siesta only lovers have alibis. And their alibis cannot be trusted.'

'And married folk.'

'Lena and Angelo? I think not. As for the Grevilles . . .'

'He told you about the blackmail.'

'Of course.'

'But . . .'

'If Signor Greville had killed the girl in order to suppress the blackmail, then he would have retrieved his cheque before her room was searched. It was not hidden?'

'Hardly. It was in the top drawer of the dressing table.'

'Exactly.' They paused.

'So how would you sum it up?'

Ferretti shrugged his shoulders. 'There is a girl whom everyone dislikes. No alibis that are really strong. In police work as opposed to detective stories one learns to start with the obvious. I cannot yet arrest Alexander Ruthven, but I shall question him more closely at Lucca. The reason is simply that his motive is the strongest. A scorned lover will always rate high. And unlike anyone else, he was seen in the car.'

'No!' said Nicholas spontaneously.

'He is your friend. I am sorry.'

'Alex will storm and swear when his vanity is hurt. But he is Don Juan. Love is a game. Murder is not a game.'

Thomas interrupted them. 'That was Ten Downing Street on the telephone. They couldn't find her.'

Nicholas made no sense of this. 'The PM? But you said she was at the Visentinis.'

'So they told me. But she left a day early. Visentini's mother died suddenly on Monday, and it was more tactful to go. So they never managed to contact her.'

'But Number Ten stay in touch with her wherever she goes.'

'This time is different. She travels under an assumed name. No London police with her. She simply gave Number Ten the name of the next convenient place where they could reach her.'

'Which was?'

'La Freddiana.'

'So she doesn't know . . .'

'She knows nothing except that she is expected to lunch. It is now half past twelve. Now, Captain, in this crisis, do you think you could send out your men on to the possible road . . .'

As Thomas spoke all three men heard a car start in the little car park adjoining the terrace. It was noisily done, and they all had cars on their minds. Nicholas ran out, in time to see the tail of the Fiat Uno belonging to the Duchess twist round the corner at the start of the steep descent. It left a spurt of dust behind.

'Someone has taken your mother's car. Whoever it is is driving helter-skelter down the drive.' Helter Skelter. Thomas stared at Nicholas as the words slipped out.

The Duchess was suddenly with them. As if she had foreseen the telephone call she wore a blazing cluster of diamonds on the bosom of an old blue dress. Unusually, she had a dab of rouge on either cheek, which made her look old and rather absurd.

'She shouldn't have called him useless.'

'What do you mean, Mother?'

135

'That girl. It was true but dangerous. Wicked, immoral, randy, yes, but not useless.'

'You mean that Dukey tried . . .'

'I wish you would not call your father Dukey. You know how he dislikes it. The day before yesterday, soon after she arrived, he went to her room. It meant nothing, it would have led nowhere, if she hadn't called him useless. As it is, poor man . . .'

Suddenly the pace of the morning changed. There was a blast of a car horn, the sound of a crash, then after a minute of confusion, the arrival of a powerful and unknown car containing familiar figures.

Of one thing, the Prime Minister, her husband and their driver were afterwards certain. As the approaching Fiat Uno hurtled off the drive and hit the wall, the expression on the face of the Duke of Stirling had been one of school-boy delight.

9
WARRIOR

It was as cold inside the armoured car as Faith could remember. She had placed herself by the tiny window, four inches by two, which looked back along the road they were travelling. The snow was piled in deep banks on either side, but on the track itself the convoys had pressed it hard into ice. The sergeant, being a veteran of Bosnia, had taken the seat at front right of the troop-carrying compartment, one foot away from a small radiator. Above his head the condensation dripped from the roof whereas above Faith's it froze.

Beyond him she could see the boots and calves of Captain Andrew Fairweather manning the Warrior's gun. He shifted and stamped, manoeuvring his feet as close to the radiator as was compatible with keeping his head and shoulders upright in the open air. It was far too noisy for conversation inside the Warrior even if the sergeant had been so inclined. In fact he was reading the latest Mary Stewart, fished out of one of the voluminous pockets of his battledress.

The only other passenger was Jim. Despite the cold he

was fast asleep, blood showing from the cut on his forehead. Not surprising that he had faded out after that ordeal. He looked thirty, whereas she knew he was forty-five. A tuft of fair hair escaped from the front of his blue woolly hat. His green and white padded jacket was attractive only to a sniper. He had always, in the four months he had been in and out of Vitez, seemed determined to look and act as differently as possible from the soldiers whose life he reported day by day. She remembered how thoroughly she had disliked him and how richly he had deserved it. As she remembered he stretched out his long legs in sleep and they intertwined with hers, knee to knee. She thought she felt, though through all those layers of clothing it must be imaginary, the warmth of his body communicating with hers.

They had met at the Christmas party. When Captain Faith Scrymgeour was not shepherding journalists on behalf of BritBat, she acted as community liaison officer with the Bosnian Croats in the Vitez pocket. The Bosnian Croats were besieged by Bosnian Muslims in the surrounding hills, and themselves besieged a tiny Bosnian Muslim enclave in Old Vitez. All of them were vulnerable to attack from Bosnian Serb artillery stationed half a dozen miles to the north.

'Siege' and 'attack' were relative words. Every few days shells and mortars would be fired, a handful of people would be wounded, a hamlet might change hands and be described in the world's press as 'strategic'. Hunger and cold were for all those concerned worse enemies than their enemies.

Faith decided on a Christmas party for Croat children in

the sergeants' mess. She rashly appointed as impresario a Guards subaltern fresh from Sandhurst. For these Catholic children Christmas was familiar, but not the English version with a performance of Ugly Sisters, novelty crackers, and blue jokes. But Father Christmas turned the tide with his generosity, and all could sing 'Holy Night'.

Faith was a sucker for Christmas. She had tears in her eyes as she watched the large-eyed children troop out into the frosty moonlight clutching their packages. The snow-covered hills were silent.

She found Jim Boater beside her. They had shaken hands at the start of the evening but there had been no time to do more than introduce themselves. She had liked the look of him, slim, wrinkles round the eyes, fair hair turning to grey, an American lumbershirt above tight jeans. She thought he might catch her mood.

But, 'Bloody farce,' he said.

'What the hell d'you mean?'

'By next Christmas the Serbs will have killed or raped half these kids. Will they thank you then for the Mars Bars and carols when the guns open up?' He pointed to the hills with their silent artillery.

'Those are Muslim guns in those hills,' she said.

'Pedantry! Heartless bloody pedantry.' Then, abruptly changing the subject, 'Where do I sleep?' He had only just arrived.

'I'll show you. Your bag's gone there.'

They crunched together through the snow, without more words. He was to sleep at the top of the rented house just outside the perimeter, in a long room converted into a dormitory for visiting journalists. Faith's room was just below – a bare light bulb, no carpet, a rather elegant green bathroom opposite, hot water stored in jerrycans in the bath. He used the lavatory on her floor, pulled the chain with violence, then stumped upstairs, kicking the wainscoting as he went.

She had met the type already. From a quality London daily, heading downhill. Angry because it was not simple, impatient of the facts he had to report, feeling the suffering at one remove, waiting for the roar of western intervention.

'Bloody cocks,' he said when they met on the stairs in the morning. He had not shaved and it did not look as if he meant to.

'There's plenty of hot water in the jerrycans in my bath,' she said. In Vitez this sounded almost romantic.

'I know exactly how St Peter felt' – as if she had said nothing. 'And he only heard it three times.'

They crossed the road, entered the perimeter, headed for breakfast. Faith had to choose between two kinds of day. Pencilled in her diary was a meeting with the Croat Mayor of Vitez, who was portly but effective. He had a scheme to reopen a kindergarten, and had found a house and a couple of teachers.

But months ago the house had been hit by a shell, whether Serb or Muslim did not perhaps matter. The Mayor wanted the Army engineers to test it for safety. She thought that he would then ask for a tarpaulin for the roof and help in cleaning, decorating, moving in furniture which had fallen off some lorry. It was a good cause, and would take most of the day. Or she could show Jim the Road. In her own mind she spelt it with a capital R, but she kept her pride to herself. She had no obligation to do this. She did not usually bother herself with single journalists.

When there was a burst of fighting, or a British soldier killed, or a Secretary of State visiting, a buzz of journalists would descend for a day, and she would drop everything else and shepherd them. Faith told herself, Jim's paper was important in a maddening sort of way, and so therefore was Jim himself.

It was the day itself that convinced her. Snow was heavy on the firs and clean on the mountains. Under the frosty sun Bosnia had shed for the day the mess and awfulness of its ordinary life, and transformed itself into a place of beauty. On such a day, the frowsty office of the Mayor of Vitez held few attractions compared with the Road.

Jim showed no sign of gratitude as they clambered into the Discovery, but he listened as they headed south. She tried to keep her voice clinical and conceal the pride she felt in what she was showing him. Gorni-Vakuf first, and the platoon of Coldstreams based in the dismal ruined warehouse between Muslim and Croat front lines. The Muslim check point, and a soldier asking to see identity papers.

'What does that red beret mean?' asked Jim.

'It means he shot a Croat yesterday who had a red beret.'

Faith regretted the remark at once. It was the sort of flip comment that she despised from others.

'No, in fact, the Muslims are the best disciplined of the three. It must be a new regiment. They're bringing fresh troops into this sector.'

Up to the Redoubt, the next army post in the woods on the ridge of mountains beyond which Bosnia fell away towards Dalmatia and the sea. The Redoubt was famous for its hot doughnuts, sticky-crackly on the outside and hot sweetness within. A deer crossed the clearing as they munched. Beyond that began the stretch of road which the Royal Engineers had created from a mountain track.

'Like the Romans.'

'It's not straight,' objected Jim. His green and white jacket was absurd.

'You can't make a mountain road straight.'

It was to her mind the right comparison. The legions built Roman roads through the mountains and wilderness of Europe, set up posts along the road, gave their own names to the landscape, defended and managed the traffic and gradually introduced the Roman peace. Only this time there was no Emperor, no law, no eagles, no triumphs through the streets of Rome, just twelve obscure Ministers sitting round tables in Brussels and New York.

They met their first convoy in mid-morning, and drew off the road to let it pass. The sun was hot by now, and the drivers were in shirtsleeves. Thin and earnest Danes, Irish from a religious charity, then five trucks from the British aid programme with hospital supplies and some generator equipment. All carried the big blue and white UN flags on the bonnets. The British were beefy cheerful drivers with tattoed forearms. One of them had met Faith before.

'What you got for us this time, love? Is it mines or mortars?' He did not stay for an answer.

Church Pond fancied itself on its cuisine. The building was a school house opposite a Catholic church with a spire, for they were into undisputed Bosnian Croat country now. The food was cooked in Chinese mode by a private from Hong Kong, and was disgusting. The striking feature of Church Pond was the sea of mud on which the whole hamlet rested.

Jim jumped out early into what looked like hard snow, and was soon well through the crust and up to his thighs in wet red mire. Faith giggled as he swore. The Discovery had to wallow its way to a sort of jetty in the sea of mud, and Faith stepped nimbly on to dry land. Jim ate bean curd while his jeans dried over the stove. His underpants were bright orange.

Finally to Tomislavgrad where the supplies accumulated from the port of Split until there were trucks to carry them into central Bosnia. An intelligence briefing by a spruce major. A quiet day, he reported, the Croatian customs being more trouble than anyone else, fussing about documents. Little real fighting this week.

On the way back Jim talked about Sarajevo fifty or so miles away, and the horrors through which he had lived. His sympathies were wholly with the Muslims. He assumed Serb responsibility for outrage after outrage. Faith had seen intelligence that told quite a different story, but she knew it would be an unprofitable argument. The UN military of all ranks and nationalities throughout Bosnia tended to quite a different view of the fighting from the journalists. Few had any sympathy for the Serbs, but few believed it was a war of right against wrong. More like a mess in which politicians and generals in all three communities destroyed their own country. Hard to explain, hard to forgive. But on the whole the soldiers kept their mouths shut, and the journalists' view swept the world.

Darkness fell on the way back to Vitez. Some of the villages had no electricity because generators had failed through lack of spare parts. In these villages the children gathered round bonfires by the side of the street until it was time to sleep. Seeing the headlights of the white Discovery, some cheered, some shouted rude challenges.

Faith felt tired but exhilarated. She did not feel much closer to Jim despite the episode of the underpants. Their talk had been professional rather than personal. But she felt she had done a good job. She left him to file his story, and went early to bed.

But she could not fight against her dreams. The slopes beyond Redoubt were a ski slope, thronged with instructors and their pupils of all ages in the bright sun. A chair-lift carried the more elderly up to a smart restaurant near the summit. Faith could see elegant ladies in dark glasses eating doughnuts. But she was following Jim down the Black Run, straining her eyes to keep his green and white jacket in sight. Then they were drinking in a smart café by the Church Pond, she cassis, he Scotch. At once she was in the bath at Vitez, enveloped in fragrant foam. The taps and the jerrycans were of gold. The door handle turned, there being no lock, and in of course came . . .

Not of course at all. Faith woke angry. It was just becoming light, and he would still be asleep, alone, in the dormitory above her head. She put on her uniform quickly and slipped out. They were surprised at the mess to find her so early for breakfast. Better to spend the day away from him.

The fax was waiting in her office when she returned in mid-morning from her talk with the Mayor of Vitez. Her secretary, a civilian from Bromley, made it a priority to get hold at breakneck speed of all stories filed by journalists who had passed through their hands. It could hardly be worse. Jim had just laughed at them all. The story was written in the worn-out pseudo-dramatic style now normal in his paper.

'British play act in Bosnia farce' was the headline. The story started with the Christmas pantomime the Ugly Sisters, the uncomprehending children.

'Equally baffling is the purpose of the whole exercise now costing the British taxpayer £200 million a year. I spent yesterday marvelling at the effort the British army is making to keep a handful of trucks rolling into Central Bosnia each day carrying Mars Bars for Croat children. The officers seem blind to the horrors a few dozen miles away. They do not make any difference between Croat, Muslim and Serb. All are patronised and scolded, for Colonel Blimp is alive and well here. The only difference is that in the modern army he is often a woman, such as my charming escort yesterday. Half the effort deployed here could have saved Sarajevo, now teetering to its inevitable fall as the world washes its hands . . .'

And so on. Slowly Faith tore up the shiny paper, shocked by the poverty of thought and expression, not yet sure how the rest of her would react.

There was no sign of Jim at lunch in the mess. As was his right, he had taken out the car and driver allocated to the press when they wanted to be independent of Army shepherding. No sign of him when dusk came. So questions were asked. He had passed through Gorni-Vakuf, but had not been seen at the Redoubt. Faith remembered having pointed out a side track which left the road short of the

147

Redoubt and led to two villages along the slope to the west. She went to bed troubled.

In the morning the driver staggered into Gorni-Vakuf. An armed group had seized the car at midday in the first of the two villages. One of them had a smattering of English. All carried sub-machine guns. After interrogating the driver they had beaten him about the head and shoved him out into the snow. He had failed to find the right tracks and staggered about aimlessly on the mountainside until he saw the broken roofs of Gorni-Vakuf.

The Colonel authorised two Warriors for the search. Faith's companion in the lead vehicle was once again Andrew Fairweather. She had met him five years ago when he was an Equerry at Buckingham Palace. He had danced well.

They reached the first village without difficulty and found the press car in the little square, its windscreen shattered. There was a small foodshop near by and various passersby, but their interpreter could get no information. Yes, there had been bad men, yes, they had attacked the car, then they had gone. Questioned about Jim, all were vague. Questioned about the direction the bad men had taken, they became contradictory.

The Warriors moved on to the second village. It was slightly bigger, and a small crowd soon gathered. Mixed Croat and Muslim, Andrew Fairweather said, though Faith was not sure how he knew. Same questions, same negative answers. The track petered out. There was nowhere else for the Warriors to go.

Andrew had an idea. It might do no good, but it could do no harm. The Warriors withdrew to the edge of the village and each fired pointblank at the rock cliff overlooking the road. The noise and the echo were tremendous. Bits of rock fell. Dogs barked and children shouted. They fired again.

'If they're around, that'll alert him and scare them.'

As if picking up the echo of the fire from the Warrior, a large bungalow on the edge of the village erupted with small arms fire. A thin figure was dodging through the garden, through a fence, sprinting along an irrigation ditch by the side of a vegetable patch. The bullets followed, he threw up his hands and collapsed into the ditch.

The leading Warrior swivelled and fired into the bungalow, once and again. A Fiat car emerged from a shed at the side and disappeared at top speed towards the main road. Faith found herself scrambling down the side of the Warrior and running towards the figure spreadeagled in the ditch. But Jim was an actor. The bullets had missed him. His only injury was a cut on the head as he fell.

'Bloody Serbs,' he said when she reached him.

'Brigands, mixed Croat and Muslim,' she replied, hauling him to his feet.

'Colonel Blimp would have left you,' said Faith twenty minutes later, seeing he was awake at the back of the Warrior. Jim opened his eyes, stared, understood, began to say something, thought better. He pretended to go back to sleep. The lock of fair hair that fell over his forehead was plastered with blood.

He edged his body forward so that his knees could continue to give his message.

10
HOME TO VUKOVAR

'**Y**our wife's pregnant?'

'Yes, Colonel.'

'Go, then. Don't hang around. Go.' The colonel spoke as if he had not on all previous occasions refused the application. He turned back to face the Danube, and raised his binoculars with gloved hands. The woods stretching down to the opposite bank of the river were leafless but for weeks had concealed death. Today the hidden guns were yet again pounding the centre of Vukovar, reducing ruins to rubble. For the moment the Serbs were leaving the water tower alone, and the Croats in this, their crucial observation post, felt momentarily relaxed.

Perhaps that was why the colonel, a difficult man, had at last given Yaroslav permission so early. Perhaps even the colonel knew that the battle was near its end. Anyway, it was proving easier than he had expected to get away. For weeks he had been summoning up the courage to play the coward. After all, Maria reminded him each evening, he was not a regular soldier. His job in the municipal engineering department had collapsed with the town's utilities.

153

For a few weeks after the siege began he had tried in a desultory way to repair shattered pumps and trailing cables, until his superior had told him he would be more use in the militia. Wrongly, for he was untrained, clumsy and short-sighted. Once in early November he trailed and shot dead a Serb sniper who had been operating from the deserted petrol station on the road south of the town. Sprawled between the pumps the Serb looked in death about seventeen. Yaroslav had thought of taking the lined jacket for it was already growing cold, but there was too much blood on it.

Now Yaroslav looked at his watch. There was not much time if he and Maria and their two suitcases were to pass through the Serb checkpoint by 4 p.m. That was the hour at which, according to the Serb military radio, their cease-fire along the Zagreb road would come to an end. The Serbs allowed six hours twice a week for Croats to leave the town and find what refuge they could in their own country. The Croatian authorities had at first barred the road, but now no longer bothered. The Serbs had surrounded the town. There was no particular purpose in further fighting. The Serbs still bombarded Vukovar each day because, Yaroslav thought, they enjoyed destruction for its own sake. The Croats held out, not because they had any hope of relief, but because Croats did not surrender to Serbs – they killed and were killed.

Yaroslav took off his militia cap and threw it into a litter-strewn patch of mud under the water tower. He did not need to hand in his uniform since he had never been issued with one. He propped up his rifle against a trestle table in the observation post, fingering for the last time the single

154

notch which marked the death of the sniper. So ended his military career.

Although there was a lull in the shelling, Yaroslav took his ancient Volkswagen round through the suburbs, rather than directly home to his village through the vulnerable centre. He passed solid houses with gardens, then two blocks of flats built in the 1960s, already streaked and crumbling by reason of weather rather than war. This part of Vukovar was lived in mainly by Serbs, as the Serb gunners across the Danube knew. Little damage had been done. Yaroslav accelerated, dodging potholes, because he wanted to get home quickly, not for any fear for his safety. These Serb civilians seemed to take little part in the war. No doubt they would line the streets and welcome the Serb tanks when finally they rolled into the town centre; but meanwhile they spent most of the time in their cellars, neither helping nor sabotaging the town's haphazard defence. Yaroslav had worked with several Serbs in the municipal engineers office, solid experienced men each looking to a reasonable pension. They had been irritated and bemused by the propaganda from Belgrade urging them to live and fight for the historic rights of Serbia. Yaroslav himself was no zealot, and Maria, being a Ruthene, was even further removed from the broadcast spasms of half-truth from both sides that fanned the fighting. Vukovar was in Croatia because Tito had put it there, though just under half of its inhabitants and most of those in the surrounding villages were Serbs. Yaroslav knew well this jumble of different churches, political parties, even alphabets, which made up Eastern Slavonia. He knew it was not possible to find a line on the map that would neatly divide Serbs from Croats, not to speak of Ruthenes and Jews. Either they

lived peacefully together, as they had under the Hapsburg
Empire, under the Yugoslav Kingdom, even under Tito – or
else the stronger coerced the weaker into subjection by
force of arms. Living peacefully together was possible, as
history and Yaroslav in his own short life had proved; but
every now and then politicians miles away decided that it
was impossible, and set the killing machines in motion
again. Yaroslav's grandfather had been bayoneted to death
fighting for the Hapsburg Empire on the Italian front in the
first war. In the second war his father had been shot by
Serbs for atrocities committed on behalf of the Gestapo by
Croat Ustachi militia. No one had seriously tried to prove
that his father was himself guilty of herding thirty Serb
women and children into a mountain cave and suffocating
them with a fire lit at the entrance; he wore the Ustachi
uniform, and that was proof enough.

'We can go,' he said, as his wife opened the door. It was
enough to see her face light up. It had often lit up like that
a year ago when they used to walk by the river in the
evening, gossiping, in love, planning marriage, watching
the old men fish and the swallows dive. There was no time
now for gossip and love. Maria had managed to see the
doctor once in her pregnancy when there had been sudden
pains. The doctor had said that she was to rest every afternoon and above all lift nothing heavy. So Yaroslav packed
the three suitcases. Clothes, the tins of food they had
hoarded for this purpose, the gilded wooden Madonna
from above their bed, his framed engineer's certificate.
Much had to be left, in particular the sticks of furniture
inherited from his parents. From the bedroom window
Yaroslav looked down the stone path lined with herbs
which led to his tool shed, lovingly built alongside the

boundary fence. A happy home, a happy garden, the house of his childhood, which for these short months had kept the latest war at bay.

As Yaroslav loaded the suitcases into the Volkswagen, Maria slipped down to the Ruthene Catholic Church at the end of the street. Of yellow stone, it proudly carried the date 1907 on its tall plain facade. The priest had left weeks ago, lamely pleading new duties in Zagreb. The church waited for whatever fate the next wave of fellow-Christian conquerors would inflict. Maria prayed briefly for the coming baby, for Yaroslav, for herself.

'You can't take these.'

'I've decided.' Yaroslav did not often say this, but when he did there was no point in arguing. He packed the almost new garden spade and fork into the back of the car alongside the suitcases. 'Wherever we go there will be soil. We shall need vegetables.' With the tools in the car and Maria beside him, Yaroslav felt reconciled to abandoning their home.

They reached the Serb checkpoint half an hour before the daily local cease-fire ended. Yaroslav did not know what to expect. At the beginning the Serbs had laughed at Croats leaving the battlefield of Vukovar and there had been cases of pillaging. Yaroslav covered the spade and fork with a strip of sackcloth brought for the purpose. But either new orders had been given, or the Serbs had begun to respect the gallantry of the hopeless defence of Vukovar. The Volkswagen was stopped, papers cursorily inspected, the family waved through.

It was otherwise at the Croat post in a wood half a kilometre further on. There the laissez passer signed by the

colonel at the water tower was scrutinised by a private soldier, then a sergeant, finally a lieutenant.

'You should join the others over there.' A military bus
was parked at the edge of the clearing. They could see it
was half full. Cardboard suitcases like their own were piled
on the roof.

'Where shall we go?'

'To Split. Accommodation will be provided there.'

'But I can drive there myself.'

'It is not permitted. The road is not safe. Take this.'

It was a receipt for the Volkswagen.

'When can I have the car back?'

The sergeant shrugged cynically. 'After the war.'

'I need these tools.'

'You will have no use for a spade and a fork in Split.'

'They are mine. I value them.'

'Comrade,' said the lieutenant, falling back into the
jargon of Tito's time, 'you have risked your life for Croatia
in the battle of the water tower. The Colonel's certificate
clearly says so. Certainly you will not grudge your country
the use of these poor tools.'

They trudged across the clearing to the bus. There was
not much talk among those inside, once it was established
that all passengers were equally ignorant of what their
future held. The bus waited until thirty minutes after the
expiry of the cease-fire, then began the long and bumpy
journey to the Adriatic.

'Yearning for revenge, would that be right?'

Yaroslav unloaded the vinegar, salt and pepper from the
tray and placed them carefully in the centre of the table-
cloth alongside the blue and yellow plastic flowers. He

disliked serving journalists because unlike NATO and UN officials they asked questions and his English was not adequate for conversation.

He had told this large English woman the night before that he came from Vukovar. Heaven knows what she was talking about now. He smiled, shook his head, and laid her place with metal knife and fork.

'Talk about bricks without straw,' Elaine muttered. It wasn't as if the food was good either. The war was over, but her paper still wanted human interest stories from the different bits of former Yugoslavia.

'Though rendered inarticulate by suffering, Yaroslav clearly yearns for revenge with every fibre of his being' she scribbled in her notebook while waiting for the thick minestrone. Not bad-looking either – he would surely agree to pose, napkins in hand, if she brought her camera to dinner. Had he mentioned a baby boy? '. . . born to bleak inheritance of anger and suffering.'

But Yaroslav was thinking of a different conversation to come, the conversation he must have upstairs once Maria had returned from the crèche and read the contents of the buff envelope which had arrived after she had left that morning. He had long rehearsed his side of the conversation, because the letter had come as no surprise – but he was not sure of Maria's reaction. It was even more difficult than he had feared.

'We should stay here.'

The notice in the buff envelope simply stated that following the victory of the Croatian Army the home registered in their name on the outskirts of Vukovar was available for immediate reoccupation. They should apply to the Resettlement Bureau before July 31 for a voucher that would entitle them to the appropriate bus fare and resettlement grant.

'Our home is there.' How could Maria think that their home could be here in Split, in this tiny hotel bedroom, with the half-efficient stove jammed into the bathroom alongside the stained bath and malfunctioning toilet?

Maria shook her head. 'Here I have a job, you have a job. Stefan is well cared for. There we would have nothing.'

'I am an engineer, not a waiter.' He hated the servility of the job, the long hours, the grubby hotel kitchen full of flies, the foreigners whom he served, not tourists nowadays, but aid officials, UN officers, journalists, all clutching a morsel of information about Former Yugoslavia and supposing it was the whole. But he could not deny the rest of what Maria had said. She cleaned at the school two streets away, was reasonably paid, and allowed to take Stefan, now nearly two years old, to toddle with other babies in the crèche and cram himself with a healthy lunch.

'You will have no job in Vukovar, engineer or waiter. Everyone says the place is still destroyed.' Everyone was the group of refugees billeted like them in the Hotel Bella Vista. The hotel had been constructed for the lower end of the Italian and German tourist trade and finished just in time for the collapse of that trade when the war began.

'There is the church waiting for you.' There was no Ruthene Catholic Church in Split that could provide Maria with the sonorous chants which had meant so much to her. But she simply shrugged.

He had shot his bolt. The things that meant much to him in Vukovar, the sweep of the Danube, the swallows of mid-summer, the path of herbs to their back door, his vegetable patch, the shed where his father had sawn logs, his mother's kitchen, all these were nothing to Maria.

'Let us at least go and have a look.' But it was a feeble suggestion. Both of them knew that if they left their room even for two days it would be occupied at once by other still homeless refugees.

'I will stay here,' said Maria. To him her tone was conclusive. He would have to stay too.

That evening the hotel manager told them that the hotel was to be refurbished for the expected return of the tourists next spring. Since Yaroslav was now listed as having a house to return to in Vukovar, he and his wife were required to vacate Room No 504 within seven days. So the argument between husband and wife had been pointless, and their wishes irrelevant.

Their own house was swept, empty, unscathed. To Yaroslav, at one level this was a great relief, but at a deeper level he knew that the house would not quickly become a home again. That would need more than the re-hanging on the wall of the wooden Madonna and the certificate from the engineering college. The break with the past was absolute; he and Maria and Stefan would have to start again.

The house next door was a charred ruin. Beyond that the Serb school teacher had remained, a widower of few words.

'What happened to the Kostic family?' asked Yaroslav, pointing to the ruin.

'They went like you, a few days later.'

'And then?'

'They came back. Three weeks ago. Also like you.'

'But – they could not live in that,' pointing to the charred beams and collapsed roof.

'The house was fine then.'

'But what happened?'

'Later there was a fire. There have been several fires. In houses to which Croats have returned. They have been unlucky.' The spectacles of the school teacher glinted sardonically.

'And the Kostic family?'

'No one was hurt. They left again.'

'Where did they go?'

The school teacher shrugged his shoulders. 'I have no idea. Croats are not welcome here.'

Yaroslav digested this. After the last five years little was a surprise.

'And who lived in our house?'

'A Serb family, from Knin. He was a farmer.'

Yaroslav understood by now the merry-go-round of ethnic cleansing. Knin was in the south-western part of Croatia where many Serbs had lived. In the last months of the war the Croat army had swept back into Knin, pushing before it a throng of fearful Serb refugees. It was natural that many of those Serbs should find refuge in the houses in Serb-occupied Vukovar from which Croats had fled months earlier. Now the UN and NATO said that both sets of expulsion had all been wrong and everyone should go back to their own homes. The Serb and Croat governments had agreed, having no choice. It must look fine on paper, Yaroslav thought. Here beside the wreck of the Kostic family home, and the comments of his neighbour, it seemed not so easy.

'That farmer who lived in my house – what became of him?'

'They were told to go. Back to Knin, I suppose.' He paused. 'So it goes on.'

The next days were not easy. The resettlement warrant given them at Split entitled the family to a certain quantity of food and fuel on return to Vukovar, financed by the UN High Commissioner for Refugees. A ticket annexed to the warrant gave the address and time fixed for an interview for Yaroslav at the Employment Bureau. But this bureaucratic precision proved to be a myth. The premises at the address given had been converted into a bar. Yaroslav walked through Vukovar street by street in search of a job. The trees on the hill and by the Danube had survived the siege better than the buildings. The town was still two-thirds destroyed. Two years of peace had brought little repair or reconstruction but a crop of flowering weeds and bushes, also food stalls and soft drink stands, among the ruins. The warm sun and full summer foliage brought cheerfulness to the scene but Yaroslav could imagine the bleakness of winter. Two restaurants and a hair-dresser had reopened, and a string of prefabricated huts beside the gutted opera house housed the school. On the hill the handsome yellow pediment of the old Academy still carried the Latin inscription that recorded its opening in the reign of the Emperor Franz Josef; but the classrooms behind that entrance where Yaroslav had studied were past repair. Swallows rested in the shattered roof; rats scurried in the rubble. Beyond the Academy, the rusting skeleton of the water tower dominated the horizon. Carnations were laid at its foot to commemorate the gallant defence of 1991.

*

Yaroslav soon discovered that Vukovar had not been gloriously recaptured by the Croatian army, as they had been led to believe in Split. It was true that the town and surrounding area, together called Eastern Slavonia, would return to Croat administration next New Year's Day. The national chequered flag already hung limply here and there in anticipation. But for the present under the Dayton Agreement the district was directly run by the UN and the joint Serb/Croat police force which the UN had recruited. The UN headquarters had been established next to the overgrown Jewish cemetery on the edge of Vukovar. Yaroslav made friends with the elderly crippled Croat who sold melons and fizzy drinks from a stall opposite the barrier at the headquarters entrance. The blue helmets were good customers off duty, and the old man held a revolving fund of gossip about the camp and its ways. When they needed to fill a job from the local community the UN first posted a notice in Serbo-Croat on a board alongside the sentry box which also provided information about the hours of water and electricity rationing and (in the early months) of curfew. Within an hour or so the same vacancy would be broadcast on the local UN-run radio and would be filled within minutes, given that unemployment in Vukovar stood at eighty per cent. The advantage lay with the qualified applicant who actually read the notice-board and presented himself in advance of the broadcast. In this way, after ten days back home Yaroslav was recruited as assistant mechanic for the varied and mostly ancient UN vehicle fleet. He was still less than he had been, a municipal engineer, but definitely more than a waiter.

Maria was not as pleased at the news as Yaroslav had hoped.

'Good,' she said, but there was no smile. She was scraping a large purple rough-leafed cabbage which was all the market had offered that morning. Stefan was well enough, but for fear of mines she did not let him run about in the garden. For the same reason Yaroslav had left it as a wilderness. Yaroslav knew that Maria was thinking of the crèche at Split, of Stefan toddling happily with the other babies, of the occasional orange or banana she had been allowed from the larder of the Bella Vista Hotel, an institution which in retrospect gained daily in splendour.

That night Yaroslav could not sleep, partly because of the stifling heat, partly because he worried about his wife's worries. They were lucky of course, compared to so many others – alive, housed, reasonably fed. He knew she had been upset by the stories of houses set on fire, and by the way the Serbs had fouled and scribbled blasphemies on the walls of the church at the end of the road. She had glimpsed a wider world, even in that dreary hotel on the Adriatic, and could not reconcile herself to the fears and hatreds of Vukovar. He watched her face turned towards him on the pillow. Moonlight touched her cheek, and added to his melancholy.

A noise in the garden took him to the window. They had nothing much to lose, but a burglar would not know this. What he saw at the end of the garden made no sense. A burly man was in the corner, near the wreck of the old tool-shed, digging quickly. The clink of his spade against a stone had alerted Yaroslav through the open window. He moved quickly down the stairs, thinking hard. Could the man be laying a mine, but why? More likely looking for something buried, a hidden possession, a body perhaps, though this village had seen less slaughter than Vukovar itself. Yaroslav had no gun, but took from behind the door the big cudgel which he had cut for Maria so that she would have some defence in his absence. His bare feet made no noise on the garden path. The big man turned, but not in time. Yaroslav hit and tripped him in the same movement before the intruder had time to raise his spade in self defence. He fell heavily, striking his head on a stone and losing consciousness for a minute. Yaroslav felt almost comic anticlimax as he looked around for an explanation. No land mine, no treasure, no corpse – just a trickle of white new potatoes from the torn soil.

'The first potatoes,' said the big man as he came round at Yaroslav's feet. 'In the eyes of God they are mine.'

'Who are you?'

'I planted them in the spring.' He raised himself on his elbow, showing no fear.

'You are the man who lived here?'

'My children have no food now.'

'But you went back to Knin.'

The Serb laughed and made to rise.

'Stay there,' said Yaroslav, raising his stick.

The Serb got up regardless.

'My name is Boris. I will not fight a man for potatoes.'

'You never went back to Knin.'

'What is at Knin? The ruin of my house which the Croat soldiers burnt to the ground. Three fields of stones, a wood. The graves of my murdered parents. It is my duty to tend the graves, and avenge the deaths. But my first duty is to my living family. There is nothing for them at Knin.'

'So?'

'So we live in a shack I built in the wood beyond the

churchyard. The bushes are thick there, and the authorities have not found us. There are six families there now.'

Yaroslav thought. Serb outcasts at the end of the street would be bad enemies. Already there was talk of the extremist White Eagle militia preparing to renew the war once the UN left. Anyway, he liked the man.

'You may keep the potatoes if you answer me a question.'

'I will try.'

'Are there mines in the garden?'

'Mines – here?'

'Some families have bought mines cheap and laid them to protect their chickens from thieves.'

'Do you take me for a savage?'

'You did not cultivate the garden, though you are a farmer.'

'We Serbs are too proud to dig. They gave me two fields and some old cows.'

'The cows are gone?'

'We live on the money I got for them.'

Later, back on the moonlit bed, Yaroslav was glad that at least men no longer killed each other for a kilo of new potatoes.

Because he worked for the UN Yaroslav had advance notice of the entertainment which the UN organised three days later in the football stadium between their village and the town. All children, Serb and Croat and Ruthene, were invited with their parents. The advertisement boldly proclaimed free ice cream and frankfurters. Yaroslav knew that the frankfurters had been flown in at great expense from a big American base in Germany. The sun shone. The stadium was only two thirds full. Despite the attractions and the sunshine, many in Vukovar were simply not yet ready for light-hearted fun with foreigners or (even trickier) with each other. The UN Administrator, Jacques Klein, had been a reserve American general. From this career he had preserved a taste for organised showmanship which he used that day to good effect. Stefan, held up by his mother, watched in admiration as the Administrator entered the stadium in a carriage drawn by four horses, preceded by a resplendent band of Pakistani pipers. He was accompanied by a silver-haired man who had, it was said, once been British Foreign Minister. The Administrator solemnly welcomed the crowd and declared the entertainment open.

For two hours Yaroslav, Maria and Stefan enjoyed themselves in a way that was entirely new to them. There were swings, merry-go-rounds and slides. Russian special troops loaded structures of brick on to the chests of their comrades. Ukrainian paratroopers swayed down from the skies. Serb and Croat children danced in their national costumes. They performed separately, but the rush for the frankfurters was in common.

Stefan was becoming tired, his face well smeared with tomato ketchup. The family decided to turn for home. As they moved towards the stadium exit Yaroslav recognised the Serb Boris bustling towards him.

'There has been a fire in your house,' Boris exclaimed, mopping the sweat from his forehead.

Maria gave a cry.

'Do not worry, lady,' said Boris. 'We saw the men, and my children and I took water from your well. There is some damage, but the fire is out.'

'This is the man who lived in our house,' explained Yaroslav, but Maria was out of hearing, dragging Stefan behind her as she hurried towards what she supposed to be the realisation of her worst fears. For Maria so far there was no reason to suppose that their lives would stop their downhill slide. So she was genuinely surprised to find their house standing and undamaged. The water from the big buckets which Boris and his grown-up sons had used had swamped the small carpet in the living room. Their half-broken sofa was badly charred and still smoking. So were the small heaps of straw which the arsonists had used to start the fire.

'They must have known you would go to the UN entertainment, so the house would be empty.'

'But how did you happen to be so close? The fire had hardly begun.'

Boris conferred in a whisper with his eldest son, then turned back to Yaroslav.

'We of course could not go to the stadium. We are non-people, registered now only in Knin. If anyone in authority had seen us . . . So for us also it was a good opportunity to come to your home again.'

'To do what?'

'Do not be stupid, Yaroslav. Please think clearly. After all, why should we come with large buckets to your garden?'

'There are still potatoes down by the tool-shed.'

'Exactly. Carrots also, and perhaps a few beans if they are not smothered by the weeds. We are still hungry.'

Maria could not follow any of this. Yaroslav had not told her of the battle of the new potatoes. She looked at Boris with deep suspicion. He was unshaven and there were tears in his coat.

'But who set our house on fire?' she asked accusingly.

169

None of them had noticed that their schoolteacher neighbour, the sardonic Serb, had joined the group.

'I can answer that. They were three youths, wearing White Eagle armbands. They were, I think, drunk. They broke into the house and lit the straw but ran as soon as they saw this man and his sons approaching. The UN police came quickly and caught them in the road a hundred metres beyond my house.'

'But how did the police know so quickly what was happening?' asked Yaroslav.

'You forget that I have a telephone,' said the teacher proudly.

'*You* rang the police?' Yaroslav was remembering the teacher's comment on the earlier fire.

'This time, yes, this time I rang them.' The teacher's glasses again gleamed. 'I thought that by now it was time to end such foolishness and lock up those drunken idiots.'

That evening Yaroslav and Maria discussed over and over again every aspect of the day's events as they mopped and cleaned the house. Finally Yaroslav put the carpet back on the dried floor.

'We should go to bed.'

'Yes, to bed.'

It was another moonlit night.

'There are no mines in the garden. I should have told you. Boris assured me.'

'Then we can grow vegetables properly, not in some Serb wilderness.'

But it was a joke. They had shared glasses of slivovic with Boris and his family before they departed.

170

'With my salary I can almost afford to buy some new tools. A spade at least, and a fork.'

They climbed the stairs in silence. Stefan was breathing easily in the cot which Yaroslav had made. A final question was necessary.

'We can stay, Maria?'

'Yes, Yaroslav, we can stay.'